PUBLISHED by PARABLES
Earthly Stories with a Heavenly Meaning

Steven Campagna

FAITH UNDER SIEGE

BY
STEVEN CAMPAGNA

PUBLISHED by PARABLES
Earthly Stories with a Heavenly Meaning

Steven Campagna

Faith Under Siege
Steven Campagna

Published By Parables
February, 2021

ISBN
Printed in the United States of America

Readers should be aware that Internet Web sites offered as citations and/or sources for further information may have been changed or disappeared between the time this was written and the time it is read.

FAITH UNDER SIEGE

By

STEVEN CAMPAGNA

PUBLISHED by PARABLES

Earthly Stories with a Heavenly Meaning

Steven Campagna

Prologue

November 1991

Pew! Pew! Shiny, silver bullets whizzed passed Ryan Hawking's right ear so close that the whoosh made him feel like his ear was locked in a tornado. The intense feeling only lasted a second though. As a soldier of the 75th Ranger Regiment of the United States, he was used to the feeling.

The American forces were fighting it out with Iraqi forces that were occupying the town of Saminga. If the Americans gained control of the small city they could stop a large supply of bombs from getting into the hands of General Saddam Hussein, the diabolical dictator who hated America and would like nothing more than to see it burn. It was Ryan's duty to make sure that didn't happen.

Zip! Zap! This time the sniper's bullet found it's target. Ryan felt intense pain unlike any other as the bullet clipped his left ear. He managed to look up just in time to see the soldier fall to the ground with a *thud.* To his left appeared a middle-eastern man by the name Ali Hussein.

Ali was originally going to be part of the Iraqi army. Saddam Hussein had requested Ali himself and he wanted the skilled warrior to be a part of his forces. But Ali knew Hussein's dark intentions and had refused. In a dark rage, the evil general had sent troops to burn down his home. He had managed to escape from the catastrophe and after barely surviving in the vast deserts and jungles, he came across some American troops that Ryan had been leading. The kind corporal had taken him to the base and got the malnourished man plenty of help. Afterwards, he and his senior officers made him an American soldier on the spot after Ali offered to do so. His story had been very moving for the troops to hear too. From the countless tales the Americans had heard of

Hussein's brutality, the story was very believable. The new recruit soon became fast friends with Ryan and the duo worked well together. Today was no exception.

Ali helped Ryan to his feet. "Are you okay my friend?"

"Always." Ryan groaned sarcastically and slowly got to his feet.

"Well I see something that will make you feel even better! Look!" Ali replied and pointed forward. Ryan looked up to see the Iraqi forces in full retreat. The Americans had won!

With renewed vigor, Ryan launched himself forward alongside Ali and mowed down two Iraqi soldiers with ease. Though it felt good to defend his beloved country against such a horrid threat, Ryan always felt a twinge of sympathy and even a little guilt for any enemy soldier he killed. He was a Devout Christian and he sometimes felt horrible for killing a soul that possibly didn't belong to Christ. Instead of ministering, he was shooting. But Ryan forced the guilt aside. He had a job to do. Plus, the Israelites had defended their own country against countless enemies in similar fashion. Ryan had every right to do the same. And with the town of Saminga and it's vast weapons supply now under American control, what could go wrong?

...

The answer came a week later. While Ryan's ear was still healing in the hospital in PA, horrible news came from the mouth of Ali Hussein.

"Evans! He's been murdered! And everyone thinks it's you who's done it!" Exclaimed Ali, gasping for breath.

Ryan was too shocked to speak. God hated cold blooded murder and as a Christian, Ryan didn't condone it either. He would never murder anybody, especially a well-known General of the United States Army!

"This is bad for you! Very bad!" Stammered Ali.

"Relax. God's in control. I'll be fine." Ryan told him. But he was also telling himself the same thing. God had gotten him out of plenty sticky situations before. But this situation was more than just sticky. It was downright awful. Ryan had hardly ever questioned his faith in God. But he had never been in a situation like this before. As soon as his friend left, Ryan began to do the only thing he could: Pray.

...

The next morning, the sun shone brightly and there was not a cloud in the sky. Squirrels and Blue Jays were gathering up some last minute nuts and acorns. Leaves of every color hung from every tree, swaying back and forth as if God himself was pushing them on a swing, as a parent does with their young child.

But despite the beauty in the world, Ryan felt the exact opposite. The cheerful call of a cardinal or the whispers of the fall winds seemed to be mocking him. Though his soul and faith remained strong, his heart was in pieces. Not so much for himself, but for his late commander Christopher Evans.

Ryan had always known Commander Evans to be an Atheist. When he had tried to preach the gospel to him after his commander had had a near death experience, the man got extremely offended and had demoted Ryan from Sergeant to Private First Class in front of the entire 75th Regiment. Since then, the duo had never been on good terms. In fact, if Evans wasn't dead, he would probably be cheering his bald head off to see Ryan in such a horrid state.
But the story of Evan's death and what he had been framed for made Ryan feel even more sick. The day after Ali had left, his lawyer, Marcus Martin had told him the story. And it was tragic and despicable. From what he knew, somebody had shot Evans in the head and had thrown his body in the river nearby. It was

cold-blooded murder and asassination. Ryan thought back to the recent conversation.

"How well did you know him?" Marcus had asked.

"Oh not that well. We talked several times."

"Any memorable instances?"

"One, yes. I tried to tell him about my belief in Christianity and the Bible. And… he didn't react very well."

"Yes, he demoted you to Private First Class, is that correct?"

"Yes. Yes it is." Ryan remembered Marcus's look of sympathy. He was lucky to have found a Christian lawyer, a brother in Christ who understood the persecution he was going through for Jesus.

Marcus had then looked up from his notepad. "Atheist?" He had asked with a slight, understanding smile.

"Yeah." Ryan had replied with the same smile.

Marcus was a burly black man with short hair and deep blue eyes. At six foot eleven he was an imposing and impressive sight. But underneath all that power was the soul of a good man who loved the Lord with all his heart and was more than ready to help a fellow believer in need.

"I want you to know that I'll do everything in my power to help you, but also remember that this case is in God's hands and he will decide the outcome." Marcus had said seriously.

"I know and I understand that. Thank you for your help." Ryan had replied gratefully.

"Anytime brother. Stay strong." Marcus answered compassionately as he stood. *"But I must be going. Joann and the kids will be waiting at home. And I don't want to miss dinner. Joann makes the best Pork Roast this side of the country!"* He had said gallantly.

Ryan had chuckled. "I'm sure she does. Thanks again and God Bless!"

"Happy to help." Marcus had replied and headed toward the door, but then he had stopped and turned. *"Have you ever thought about getting married? I'm sure you'd be quite the catch."* He had finished with a sly smile.
"Oh not really. I guess it's something I just never really had thought about. After all, I'm only twenty three years old, there's plenty of time for me." Ryan had joked.

"I suppose that's true brother. I suppose that's true." Marcus had replied.

Ryan had only hoped he would have the chance to have a family, instead of being on death row.

...

Throughout the proceedings, every witness seemed to feel that because Evans had demoted Ryan in front of the entire regiment, he had a desire for revenge. Ryan knew it was false and he knew for a fact that God knew it too. As a Christian, he had no bloodlust.

Unfortunately, the Supreme Court of Delaware seemed to think differently. In the end, Marcus was able to get Ryan out of being executed, but the once great American soldier still fell prey to a one hundred year sentence in Delaware State Prison.

Wham! When the wooden mallet slammed down on the Judge Cooper's table, it felt like the blow had shattered his soul. As the guards led him away, Ryan casted a sorrowful glance at Marcus who nodded slowly and in Mariana Trench-deep empathy.

Is this the life that God had planned for him? A life locked away in a cell? Was he to be a Christian who would go through life suffering behind steel bars and missing out on the opportunity to save souls for Christ? Where was the hope in that? There didn't seem to be any whatsoever.

...

A few days, Ryan had his first visitor: Ali Hussein

"I can't tell you what it's like to be on this side of the glass." He murmured to his friend sadly.

"You have my sympathy. I too find it difficult to imagine you as a killer." Ali had replied sorrowfully.

"Well, don't worry about me. God's-"

"-in control." Ali finished. Ryan looked up in surprise.

"Your lawyer, Mr. Martin... we got the chance to talk about your belief in God. And...everything he said made sense to me! He told me things about God I had never even thought possible! But I feel they're true! And last night...I accepted him as Lord and Savior of my life."
Ryan Hawking's eyes teared up with pure joy at the news. There was hope! God was still at work!

"I wish you well old friend. Stay strong in your faith. If I have the time, you can count on my return!" Ali stayed enthusiastically.

"Glad to hear it! God bless you!" Ryan replied with the same enthusiasm.

The two men exchanged a quick prayer before Ryan was led back to cell three. Though it was an extreme hardship to be away from the rest of the world, Ryan Hawking now had no doubt that there was still hope and healing for a broken world that desperately needed Jesus Christ, the one true God. And one day, he would return to make all wrongs right.

But until that day came, Ryan would continue to pray for the millions of souls who were lost. Being locked in a jail wasn't going to be much of a life, but Ryan understood that it was the life God had chosen for him. Why? To him, it didn't make much sense. But as a devout Christian he knew full well that God's ways were higher than his. And because of that, Ryan Elias Hawking was ready to follow God's road, wherever it took him.

1

November 2019

Beep. Beep. Beep. Charlie Boxford's alarm clock went off at 8:45 AM.

"Church is today!" The fourteen year old boy thought excitedly. His father, David, was the head pastor and founder of *Boxford Baptist Church* located in Collingswood, South Jersey, and would be delivering another sermon. Charlie loved to hear his father preach. The passion of which he spoke of Jesus and the Bible gave Charlie the same fervor made him want to serve God in the same way.

But there was one problem: Charlie wanted to be like his father and serve God by preaching, but he was afraid to do so. Charlie didn't feel he could possibly handle such a job. He had never told his father of his feelings. He didn't want to disappoint him. He had disappointed enough people already, including four people who had just-

"No. I won't think about them." Charlie thought vigorously to himself. *"They're gone and I have to move forward."*

As Charlie got himself dressed, he thanked God for his blessings and began humming one of his favorite hymns: *How Great Thou Art.* He had gotten the gift of singing from his mother, who had made it into the South Jersey Chorus a couple years ago.

He was small for age fourteen, only four and a half feet tall, and sometimes his small size made him insecure. Shyness was another trait he'd inherited from his mother, only she'd been able to overcome it. Charlie wished he could find it easy to do the same.

But there were some things he hadn't inherited from Louise. His love for science, specifically Physics, was one of them. His MK One Homemade Catapult, *Hammerhead,* was finally ready for testing!

"I've got time before breakfast to give Hammerhead a go." He thought cheerfully to himself. Two things always made Charlie Boxford happy: God and Science. After reading *The Sermon On The Mount,* which he did every morning before he began his day, he went downstairs to test *Hammerhead.*

...

Beep. Beep. Beep. Marcy Boxford's alarm clock went off at 8:45 AM. Her first thought upon waking was the same as her brother.

"Time for church." Only Marcy wasn't excited about it. For her, church wasn't a secure, friendly, and reassuring place. It was a place where people pointed out her faults and made her feel uncomfortable. What made matters worse was that her own father led them all.

She had used to trust her parents a lot. But as she got older, they had begun holding her back and not letting her do anything. Her father was overprotective and her mother, a woman who she had formally admired so much, didn't stand up to him. Instead, she just let the man of the house rail on her. The seventeen year old girl had questioned her mother about the issue just yesterday. She remembered the conversation. It hadn't exactly gone very well:

"Mom, can you please tell Dad I just want him to leave me alone?"

"I'll tell him. But he doesn't want you hanging out with those kids. And neither do I for that matter."

"I know. It's just… I feel more at home with them then here." Marcy remembered the shocked look on her mother's face.

"Marcy, sweetheart we're your family! You should feel safest here!"

"I used to… not anymore."

"Well why is that?"

"I don't want to tell you. It'll just upset you."

"Maybe, maybe not. But I can't help you if

you don't tell me what's wrong." "I know.

Just please tell Dad to let me be with my

friends okay?"

"Your father doesn't want you near them and honestly, I'm inclined to agree with him. And besides, even if I did disagree with him it's not my place to argue with his decisions."

"Why? If anyone can convince him of anything it's you!" Her mother had nodded in reply.

"That may be true, but as a Godly wife, I must submit to the man of the house, whether I, You, or your brother likes it."

Marcy had been utterly appalled at her mother's words. She had always known her mother to be the strongest woman she knew- her ultimate role model. Who was this… submissive weakling? "What?! Just because he's a man?!"

"Yes."

"Mom, that's sexist!" She had yelled.

"No it's not! It's the way God made marriage to be!"

Her mother had replied angrily. "But-"

"We're done with this conversation young

lady. Now go clean up your room." "But Mom,

you always taught me to be strong!"

"When we obey God's rules we become all the stronger. He's made me stronger than I've ever been."

Marcy had just sighed. It hadn't made sense. It still didn't. "Well I'm not going to submit to any man!" She had yelled.

"Then good luck having God's approval." Her

mother had replied. "Now go-" "I don't care

about his approval or Dad's! I'm living my

own life!"

"You'll live by God's rules as you're living under this roof young lady!"

"No I'm not!"

"Marcy Catherine Boxford you will go clean up your room this instant or-"

"Or what?! God's gonna send lightning out of the sky and strike me dead?! Ohhh, I'm terrified Mom! I really am!" Marcy had responded sarcastically.

Whap! Her mother had slapped her in the face. "How dare you speak to me that way?! God is the master of this house! If you don't like it, then go and live out on the streets for all I care!"

Tears had come to Marcy's eyes and she had run upstairs crying. She had flopped down on her bed sobbing and didn't get her room cleaned up until much later. She had gone to bed a little later without a word to her family.

...

Marcy just didn't understand it. So what if some of her friends smoked and cursed? They cared about her. All her parents did was yell at her. *"Jesus died for everyone. If we don't sin a little, then Jesus died for nothing."* She thought to herself. She knew who Jesus Christ was. She lived in a Christian Household, how could she not? But since she was old enough to understand, the idea of having a God looking over her seemed alien and even a little creepy. As a young lady, she needed her alone time. Obviously, her family's God didn't respect that. *"Well duh! Of course he wouldn't! My family doesn't respect that either!"* She grumbled as she dressed herself.

She had "accepted Christ" when she was ten, when in reality she just went through the motions to please her family. And what did they do in return? Spit in her face. And submit to a man?! Absolutely not! Marcy knew how to fight and had the utmost respect of all the boys in her school. Even the seniors admired her! Marcy knew it took a special girl to get that kind of attention. She wasn't about to give it up.

After tidying up her silky blond hair in a neat ponytail she looked at the reflection in the mirror. "You're going to live your life girl. Whether God, your father, or anybody else likes it or not, you're living your own life."

Marcy took a deep breath and headed downstairs for breakfast. "You got this." She told herself, when in reality she wasn't so sure. But she was sure of one thing: She didn't need a God.

2

Marcy stomped down the wooden stairs just as Charlie was testing *Hammerhead.* Charlie loaded a small, plastic ball into the catapult.

"Ready… aim… fire." He murmured to himself and let the ball fly… whap! Right into his sister's right shoulder.

...

Marcy yelped and stepped back in shock. Wincing in pain, she looked at her shoulder. A black and blue bruise was on it. It was small but it still hurt. She already had to go to church. As if her day wasn't bad enough all ready!

"I can always count on my idiot brother to make things worse!"

She scowled silently to herself. ...

Charlie gulped as his sister glared at him. Marcy was almost a foot and a half taller than him and even though he was fourteen and not five, he couldn't help being a little worried. "I'm so sorry! I didn't hear you coming!" He said calmly.

"Yeah. Sure." Marcy said grumpily.

"I'm telling you the truth Marcy! Do you want me to get you a band aid or something?" He asked gently.

"What?! Do you really think I'm that weak?! I can

take a hit!" Marcy yelled at him. "Hey, I was just

trying to be nice!" Charlie protested.

"Oh bull Charlie! You always like to pull this sort of stuff!" Marcy replied.

"What stuff?" Charlie asked, exasperated. What was Marcy's deal?

"Don't play dumb, you know what I'm talking about! You hurt me or break something and because I'm older I still take the blame!"
"What?!" Now Charlie was mad too. "I've never hurt you on purpose! Ever! And I'm not seven, I'm fourteen! I shoulder plenty of blame too! Mom and Dad expect just as much Godly character from me as you!"

"Don't you dare yell at me!" Marcy growled threateningly.

"Then don't act like a turd!" Charlie shouted back at her.

"I can act how I want to!"

"That's not what Jesus would say Marcy."

"You think I care?!"

"As a Christian, you should." Charlie replied worriedly. Marcy had always not shown much spiritual fruit, but she had never said she didn't care about Jesus before. It concerned him greatly. Had his sister left the faith?

"You have no right to correct me Charlie! In case you've forgotten, I'm three years older than you!" Said Marcy and took a step towards him.

Charlie held his ground. "Then act like it!" He growled.

Wham! Marcy pushed him backwards and he fell. Whack! The back of his head hit the edge of the kitchen table. "Ow! What's your problem?" Charlie asked as he stood up holding his head.

"You and everyone else!" She growled and reached for him.

"Hey! Break it up!" Said a voice from behind. The sibling's father stood on the steps gazing angrily at the both of them.

"She started it!" Charlie said instantly.

"I did not! He did!" Marcy protested.

"I don't care who started it, I'm ending it!" Their father said. "Responsible teenagers. That's who I thought lived in this house. But now I think I have a couple of five year olds in teenage bodies!" He scolded.

"What is with all the ruckus?" Their mother asked as she

followed her husband down the stairs. "He's being a brat again!"

Marcy called.

"I am not!" Charlie retorted.
"It sounds to me like you both are!" Louise stated, disappointment clearly a feeling in her voice. She turned to her daughter. "I had hoped things were going to go better than yesterday." She said coldly.

"Well, life is full of disappointments." Marcy replied, her normally sweet voice filled with a boatload of snobbery.

Charlie was shocked! So were his parents. Both he and Marcy had been snotty with their parents before, but Marcy had just taken everything to a whole other level.

"You will apologize to your mother...now." His father growled at her, his dark green eyes full of rage.

"Fine. Sorry." Growled Marcy and looked away.

"Well, you have lost car privileges for the whole next

week." Her father stated plainly. "Whatever." Marcy

growled.

After a short silence Louise spoke up. "Well on that pleasant

note, let's have some breakfast." ...

The breakfast was Charlie's favorite: pancakes and waffles. But the tension between family members hung over the wooden table like a thick black cloud, just waiting to devour the rest of the day in a single demonic gulp.

...

And the cloud was satisfied. During the car ride nobody spoke to each other. And church wasn't much better. As David Boxford preached a sermon on love, he couldn't help noticing the hatred and disunity within his own household. It broke his heart and darkened his soul that the head pastor of *Boxford Baptist Church was* struggling to keep his own family from falling apart.

...

After the sermon, David went up to one of the deacons of his church who was a good friend of his: Ali Hussein, a Desert Storm Veteran who had come to know Christ after a fellow believer, Ryan Hawking, had told him about Christ shortly before before prosecuted to jail for the rest of his life for a crime he hadn't committed. David and Ali continued to pray for him and countless
others whenever possible. Ali was a brand new American when he had first arrived. He was looking for a church to go to and when David had met the man, he had asked him if he knew of any possible churches he could attend. David had smiled, and right then and there, Ali would find his church.

David went up to his friend and shook his hand firmly. "How are you?"

"Pretty well, thanks." Ali responded happily. "How's the family?"

David sighed sadly as he watched Marcy and Charlie depart their mother and head outside for the youth group. "It could be better with Marcy. She's…stubborn."

Ali just smiled. "Aren't all teenagers?"

David chuckled. "That's true. But I honestly thought being a Godly father would've been at least a little easier."

"Nothing about the Christian life is easy, pastor. You know that. I

mean, you've preached on it!" "I know."

"And you know what God's called you to do, don't you?"

"Yes."

"And are you willing to follow him and trust him with all your heart?"

"I am."

"Then you're all set!"

David smiled, feeling better already. "Thanks Ali.

Your encouragement means a lot." "Would it help if I

prayed with you about Marcy?"

"Yes it would."

"Then let us pray to him who helps all." Ali said gallantly and the two friends began to pray.

3

Meanwhile, Marcy and Charlie had headed outside for the youth group.

"Hey Marcy wait up!" Charlie called after her. He

wanted to make things right with her. "What?" Scowled

Marcy, turning to face him.

"Ummm… look about earlier, I'm-"

"I don't want to talk about it." She interrupted coldly.

"But I just wanted to say-"

"Look, I just said I didn't feel like talking about it!"

"For Pete's sake Marcy, do you honestly have to be so rude? I'm just trying to-"

"I don't care, just shut up!" Marcy exploded. Charlie stepped back and gulped nervously as everyone turned to look at him and his sister. This wasn't going the way he had hoped at all.

"Hey Marcy, do you want to talk about the issue with me alone?" The kids turned to see the face of one of their youth leaders, Mrs. Joann Scotts, looking at Marcy compassionately.

"Yeah, sure." Marcy sighed and walked over to her. But she turned to glare at him one more time. "I'm gonna get you for this you little rat." She growled menacingly. Charlie stepped back again. Marcy just laughed. "Scaredy-cat." She said and walked off with Mrs. Arnold Scotts.

Charlie hadn't realized he was shaking until then. He was relieved when another youth leader, Mr. Rick Owens, called for the attention of the group.

...

After the group, Charlie felt a tap on his left shoulder. He turned to see Katie Scotts looking down at him. Katie was one of Marcy's closet friends and because the nineteen year old had babysat him often when he was younger, Charlie saw her like another older sister. Although he had never admitted it to her or anyone, Charlie sometimes still missed being the five year old that Katie was so gentle with. But he was fourteen now, and the childhood years were over. But Katie had still remained a great friend and Charlie was still just as close with her as he was before. In fact, Katie knew him well enough to know when something was wrong. But after his attempted apology to Marcy had gone so awry, the teenager knew it didn't exactly take a rocket scientist to tell that there were issues in the household. "Hey, How you doin'?" Katie asked and ruffled his hair.

"Bro, I told you stop doing that." Charlie replied

playfully and pushed her hand away. "I must've

forgotten." Katie stated sarcastically, raising her

hands in surrender.

"So how's *Harry?*" He asked. *Harry* was her pet Iguana. Charlie found him super cool. Katie stared at him playfully.

"So you don't ask how my parents are, you don't even ask how I am, you ask me how my pet Iguana is. Wow, Charlie I thought I raised you better than that." She said and started poking him.

"Alright I'm sorry!" Charlie laughed. "It's just he's really cool."

"And I'm not?"

"Oh no you are. Just not as cool as him." Charlie teased her.

"What?"

"He never treats me like I'm still five in front of my friends." Charlie joked. "Well who read you *Jack And The Beanstalk* a thousand times a day?" She retorted. "You did."

"Who let you cuddle with them when you were scared of a thunderstorm?" "You did."

"And who got you French Fries from McDonald's for you when you begged for them?" "You did."

"Besides, your parents and Marcy, who practically raised you?"

"You did." Charlie said and chuckled at the memories.

"So considering that a little reptile never could do any of those things, I'd say I'm way cooler." "But he's a marvel of science!" Adam protested.

"Well, I'm a marvel of God who created science!" Katie shot back.

"So am I!" Charlie said.

Katie took a step towards him. "I am…inevitable. She said sharply and snapped her fingers. "Hey you know I can't snap my fingers! That's cheating Katie!" He growled playfully. "Not my fault if you'd be a horrible Thanos." She joked.

Charlie sighed. "I just wish I wasn't a horrible brother."

Katie's gaze softened. "What happened kiddo?" She asked gently.

"Remember I was telling you about *Hammerhead?*"

"Yeah, your catapult, I remember you had it almost completed too."

"Well I completed yesterday and decided to test it this morning. But-"

"The projectile hit her and she flipped." Katie finished for him. Charlie looked up at the brown-haired girl in surprise. "As soon as you mentioned *Hammerhead* I had a pretty good guess of what happened." Charlie smiled. It always made him feel better to talk to Katie. "Don't worry about it Charlie. I'm sure she'll be over it later." She said and kissed his hair. Charlie blushed and he saw some of his guy friends chuckling to themselves and looking in his direction.

One of them, Ethan Parker, called out: "Yo Charlie's into them older girls!" Charlie laughed as Katie gave him an angry look.

"That's why I keep telling you not to treat me like that in front of them." He said. "Well I know you miss it." Katie replied mischievously, a teasing look in her hazel blue eyes. "Nah."

"Yes you do." She stated. "And it's a sin to lie." She whispered

in his ear. Charlie sighed as he found himself reminiscing

about the past. "Okay fine. I admit it. I miss it."

"I knew you did. But I'm proud of how far you've come. I know
you sometimes think that you're too small and weak to be
brave, but I disagree. You're a very brave boy." She said
warmly.
"Of course you'd say that." The words came out a little
harsher than he meant. He looked at Katie. "I'm sorry I
shouldn't have snapped at you. It's just…" Charlie's voice
trailed off.

"You're grieving Charlie. I understand. And I know you blame
yourself for what happened to them. But you can't do that and
deep down you know I'm right." Katie encouraged him gently as
they walked towards her car, a bright red 2015 Ford Focus that
was previously owned by her mother.

"Yeah, I know. But it was my idea."

"And God knew you'd have it and he let you speak it. If it
wasn't part of his perfect plan he wouldn't have let you
speak." Charlie nodded, taking in the wisdom of his nineteen
year old friend.

"Yeah I know that too. And I'm willing to trust in him." He said,
surprised by the confidence in his voice.

"Then you're all set. Stay strong Charlie. I love you." Katie
murmerd proudly and kissed his hair again. This time Charlie
didn't protest in any way. He was just happy that Katie cared
about him so much. Not many people had a friend like her, that
was for sure!

"Thanks. I love you too. And thanks for the help."

"Anytime. Well… I have to get to work. I'll see you later okay?" She said as she opened the car door.

"Yeah I'll see you around!" Replied Charlie. "Oh hey wait I forgot something." He said suddenly and rushed toward her. He gave Katie a big hug. Katie embraced him warmly. "I love you Katie. Thanks for everything." He whispered.

"I love you too Charlie. You're a good boy." She said as she released him. And with that, Charlie watched her drive off. He heard some of his friends snickering behind him but he didn't care. All that mattered to Charlie Boxford was that he knew he had a special person, and an even more special God, that loved him and would continue to look after him.

4

Meanwhile, Marcy was talking with Katie's mother, Joann Scotts. "I couldn't help noticing the tension between you two this morning."

"I don't think anybody couldn't notice." Marcy sighed.

"Maybe so, but it's sad to see you two fight when you're normally so close." Mrs. Scotts replied. "I guess we haven't been as close lately."

"For how long?"

"A couple months."

"Let me guess. Ever since your-"

"Yes. Since they died." Marcy interrupted. Mrs. Scotts gave her a surprised look. "I'm sorry. I just...don't want to talk about them."

"Talking sometimes helps." Mrs. Scotts reasoned.

"Mrs. Scotts, I'm just not ready yet." Marcy explained, an exasperated look on her face.

"That's fine." Stated Mrs. Scotts calmly, raising her hands in surrender. "But one thing that I know is true is that the toughest times, a sibling can be your greatest ally."

"Well, don't get me wrong, I love Charlie, it's just...he doesn't know his place. He thinks he's in charge of me and he's not." Marcy explained.

Mrs. Scotts stopped walking and turned to face her. "Marcy sweetie, I'll let you in on a little secret: Every man, older or younger, will always behave like that around you."

Marcy chuckled. "I don't think that's any secret Mrs.

Scotts." She said with a smile. "Maybe so. But you

know your brother has good intentions right?"

"Yeah."

"And you know he just wants to protect you because he loves you right?"
Marcy laughed at that. "Charlie couldn't protect me from someone even a little younger than him if he tried."

"Marcy..." Mrs. Scotts gasped scoldingly.

"Well it's true! He's tiny and has no self confidence!" Marcy retorted.

"Well maybe you could help him get there instead of

criticizing him." Mrs. Scotts replied. "I already tried that."

"What did you do?"

"I invited him to hang out with my new friends but he just judged the things they did until we exploded at him and he ran home."

Mrs. Scotts nodded slowly. "Are these new friends of yours the same kids your father doesn't want you hanging out with?" She asked, a knowing look in her hazel, blue eyes.

"At that time they weren't because my father didn't know I was around them. But of course, the little "angel of the house" just had to go and blab to Mom and Dad about all the horrible and Ungodly things he saw them do. And ever since then, my parents have been trying to eliminate my best comfort source!" Marcy explained to her.

Mrs. Scotts nodded thoughtfully. "I can see how that would be upsetting for you Marcy. When did you start hanging around with these kids?"

"A few days after...the passing of...you know."

"Okay. I recommend using God as a comfort source. He's-"

"I don't need him." Marcy said quickly.

Mrs. Scotts looked utterly flabbergasted.

"Marcy... everyone needs God." "Not me.

I'm through with him." Marcy stated coldly.

"But Marcy, you've always had a good faith in God! When times are toughest, that's when you need to trust him most!"

"Mrs. Scotts...I was never what you church folk call 'saved.' I only accepted Christ to please my family, especially my father." Marcy admitted. *"And apparently even that wasn't good enough."* She thought silently to herself.
Mrs Scotts was just standing there, looking shocked. It was as if not being a Christian was some sort of evil deed, a horrid crime. "Marcy...I..."

"Please don't explain Mrs. Scotts. I've been through a lot lately and I don't need somebody else just staring down at me waiting to pounce on me every time I mess up."

"Honey, God's not like that! His mercies are new every morning and his compassion never ends! It says that in the book of Lamentations!"

"Mrs. Scotts I'm glad you have such a strong faith in God, I really am, but religion just isn't for me."

"Sweetheart your father's the head pastor of this church! How do you think he would feel if he knew that own daughter was in rebellion against his God?"

Marcy took a deep breath, trying to hold back her tears. "Then he'd have to decide who he loves more: Some God that may or may not even exist, or his own daughter. The same goes for my mother."

"What about Charlie?" Mrs. Scotts asked.

"Charlie is an annoying little brat that is trying to ruin my life. I honestly don't care what the little termite would think!" Marcy spat angrily.

"And what about me and Katie?" Mrs. Scotts questioned her.

"I...don't know." Marcy sighed. "I'm just tired of feeling like I have to be perfect or some God is going to crush me."

"Marcy, God loves you more than anyone! He's not going to crush you. Don't get me wrong, he'll correct you, but if you obey him and trust him, I promise he will always forgive you and-"

"Mrs. Scotts please!" Marcy begged. "I'm really glad following God still works for you but it was honestly never for me! I'll always love you and Katie but this my choice, okay? I just want to stop feeling like I'm under siege twenty four seven three sixty five!"

"Marcy God will help you not feel that way if you let him help you!"

"Mrs. Scotts I don't need another sermon!"

"Marcy I'm just trying to-"

"I know what you're trying to do Mrs. Scotts and I thank you, I really do. But I don't need a God."
"What do you need?" Mrs. Scotts asked her.

"To be left alone." Marcy replied coldly.

"Marcy-"

"Thank you for your time Mrs. Scotts." She said and walked away, wiping the tears from her face the whole time.

...

Charlie watched Marcy walk away from Mrs. Scotts. He had hoped to talk to his sister again, but now obviously wasn't the time.

Suddenly, a hand clasped him on his shoulder. Charlie turned to see Mr. Hussein staring at him happily.

"How have you been, young man?"

"Not gonna lie I've been better. How about you?"

"Pretty good actually. And I know what happened with Marcy earlier." He said, nodding to his father.

"Yeah..."

"I'm sure she'll be fine. She's been through a lot lately as have you. Just give her space." Mr. Hussein advised him.

"Thanks I will."

"Well I have to go soon, but do you have any other questions for me?"

Charlie grew thoughtful. "I do have one actually."

"Fire away."

"Why are women so confusing?" Mr. Hussein and his father

broke down laughing. "That's definitely one of the top ten

questions scientists still can't answer." Mr. Hussein joked.

"Too true. That's a question only Father God knows the answer to." His father put in with a smile.
"Then I guess we'll have to wait and see what he says. And honestly, I'm looking forward to it." Charlie joked with them. His father and Mr. Hussein chuckled with him.

"Hush now. Here comes your mother with the car." His father said.

"Well I'd best be going. It was a pleasure to see you again Charlie." Said Mr. Hussein gallantly and extended his hand.

"You too sir. I'll see you next week." Charlie replied and shook it firmly.

"Not a word to your mother now." Said his father.

"Yes sir." Charlie replied and the family drove away from church and headed home. The whole time Charlie silently thanked God for making him such a Godly young man and prayed that he would continue his work in him. But Charlie also prayed for Marcy, who wasn't Godly and needed help. Charlie made a vow that if his sister needed him, he would be there for her no matter what.

5

Once the family arrived home, business went on as usual. That evening, Mr. and Mrs. Boxford left to go to dinner at a nearby diner. The parents had kept the tradition of a husband-wife bonding time without the kids every Sunday night.

"We'll be back late tonight! Get to bed before nine because it's a school night!" Marcy's mother called to her and Charlie as she left with her father.

"Okay." Said Charlie.

"Yeah, sure." Shrugged Marcy and stalked off to her

room without saying goodbye. ...

At the *Medport Diner,* David and Louise were happily eating together.

"I still remember how we first met. Do you?" Asked David.

"I try not to." Relied Louise, mischief

sparkling in her dazzling green eyes. "How

about I remind you?" David teased.

"It was warm, sunny day at work and without warning, this

striking blond buety strides in-" "Oh! Stop it!" Louise

interrupted, blushing big time.

"And she asks me 'Do you know where the bathroom is?'"

"This was the most embarrassing moment of my life." Louise murmerd, half to herself.

"It was embarrassing for me too because my mother had locked herself in the bathroom and could not get out and had started screaming for help." David exclaimed with a laugh.

"I still don't understand how she locked herself in

a public stall." Louise chuckled. "True. But the girl

just happens to be so nice and she helps her

escape."

"And that's because the 'girl' was currently working in a nursing home and had dealt with problems like this before."
"And after she saved my poor mother, she said she'd hope to see me again. She had already liked me." David bragged.

"Well, you were quite the stallion back then." Louise admitted.

"Just back then?"

"Yes, just back then! The lean and ripped stallion I used to know has decided to become a hog! Just look at you!" Louise said, playfully mocking him and pointing at his stomach.

"Now this baby here has expanded for one reason and one reason only: I'm looking at that reason." Said David, staring straight at her.

"My pork chops are worth it are they not?"

"Totally. I've been telling you to go *Chopped* you know."

Louise shook her head. "I'm just not that good

around that sort of pressure honey." "Oh alright. I'm

just glad there's no pressure on either of us here."

"Do you think we were too hard on Marcy? She's only been
acting like this since the plane went down."

David looked thoughtful for a moment then shook his head no.
"Not honoring your parents is not honoring your parents. Sin is
sin Louise. We did the right thing." David stated reassuringly.

"I'm glad to know you're confident about that. It's hit them both
pretty hard." Louise said.

"David nodded his shiny, bald head in agreement. "And they
obviously grieve differently too. Marcy explodes in anger,
pain, and fear, and Charlie tries his hardest not to talk or
probably even think about them."

"Well since they're teenagers they're trying to figure out
themselves as hard as we try to figure them out ourselves."
Louise put in.

"I agree with you completely. I remember being their age well.
It's not an easy time as it is and throwing in a death in the family
makes it even more stressful." David added.

"Absolutely. I certainly wouldn't go back to my teenage
years. I remember feeling like I was constantly under siege
all the time." Louise said.

"Same here."
"And because we're Christians, our faith is under siege all the
time."

"But he who is in us is greater than he that is in the world."

"1 John 4:4." The couple quoted at the same time.

"Amen." They said at the same time and burst out laughing with glee.

...

Back at home, things unfortunately weren't as cheerful. Charlie had asked Marcy if she wanted to hangout with him, but his sister had just simply ignored him as if he didn't exist. And so, he decided to put some upgrades on *Hammerhead.* When he finished almost an hour later, the catapult looked grander than ever.

...

Upstairs in her bedroom, Marcy was content watching her favorite show: *Grey's Anatomy.* She longed to be a doctor or nurse so she could help people one day. She wasn't the type of girl to help people to get a reward out of it, she just plain liked doing it. It was part of her being a good person. But why couldn't her own family, the people she was formally the most close with, see
that she was a good person? And even more confusing, and seemingly selfish, was the way that her family viewed everybody else who wasn't a Christian. They said things that seemed very arrogant, offensive, and even a little discriminatory. For example, she remembered hearing her father say in one of his sermons that the only way to get to heaven was to be a Christian. It had scared her to hear her father say such a thing. So much so, that even though she hardly even understood what she was doing, she had "accepted Christ" that night.

But that had been when she was only ten years old. She was older now. She was stronger, smarter, and wiser. And she was old enough to know who she wanted to hang out with, who to trust, and who not to trust. And she also believed that she knew what she wanted to do with her life and that certainly did not include following a judgemental God who seemed to only like people who were like the rest of her family. As for everybody else, who cared about them? If somebody wasn't a perfect, holy Christian, they should be thrown into hell! Marcy didn't want to live a life like that.

A soft *ding* from her purple phone interrupted her deep thoughts. Her secret relationship, a seventeen year old boy named Matthew "Hooper" Fenton, had just texted her. He was nicknamed "Hooper" because he was so good at basketball. In fact, he had broken several records at school. Marcy had found the stocky young man attractive since freshman year. But she had had no clue that he had felt the same way about her until he had asked her out earlier in Junior Year. She had known even then that her parents wouldn't approve of him. But she didn't care. Matthew Fenton was the nicest boy she had ever met and she had quickly become obsessed with him.
"U wanna hang out with me and the bros at Freedom?"
Freedom was the name of a nearby park.

Marcy sighed sadly and texted him back:

"Can't. Grounded. Took car keys." A few

moments later he texted her back: *"I'll come*

get u I don't mind."

"Parents would kill me."

"Do they know about us?"

"No"

"Then what's holding u back?"

"Charlie's still up."

"He still workin on that stupid catapult?"

"Yeah, hit me in my shoulder earlier today. Little brat."

"Want me to beat him up for u?" He replied. Marcy almost said yes but she still loved her brother enough to not put him through such a thing. Plus, she'd never hear the end of it from her parents, topped off with some kind of horrid, never-ending punishment. Marcy didn't need that.

"Nah still my little bro."

"Gotcha. Want me to come get U? I can come over right now."

"Don't know. Parents will most likely be out

late but I don't know for sure." "I'll come

get u."

"My parents Mattie…"

"So what hot stuff? They won't know. Cmon baby. For me?"

"Maybe."

"Well guys over here getting impatient u coming? If u are, wear something hot." Marcy blushed as she read the text.

"I'm hot period Mattie u know that."
"Yeaaaah baby."

"I love u Mattie."

"I love u too. Last shot: 5min away. Want me to come get U?"

Marcy stared at the text. She knew it was wrong what she wanted to do, but Matthew made her feel so good about herself. He loved her for who she was, not who other people said she should be.

She felt safe around him. He was loving, supportive, funny, muscular, brave, and handsome
as could be. He was everything a girl like Marcy could want. Nevertheless, her parents made the rules, and if she went against them, she knew for a fact if they found her out, she would have many more problems. But Matthew treated her better than anyone including her family. How could she possibly make such a hard choice. For almost thirty seconds, she had no clue. But after that, she knew what she wanted to do. She answered Matthew's text.

...

Thwip! Thwip! Thwip! Charlie watched *Hammerhead* proudly as the catapult launched three more balls in perfect unison. It had taken a lot of work to get the catapult where it needed to be, but it had been well worth it. *"For what a man sows he will also reap."* Charlie thought happily to himself.

Charlie looked at the clock. *"8:15 already! Time to get ready for bed!"* He thought and quickly headed upstairs to take a shower.

...

Once in bed, Charlie found himself quickly getting tired. He was just falling asleep when he thought he heard the front door open. He was almost too tired to check, but he willed himself to stand. It couldn't have been his parents. They weren't supposed to be home until late. As he left his room, he heard a car drive off. As he passed Marcy's room he found her door open. He looked inside...and the room was empty. Marcy was gone.

6

"What the heck?! Where'd she go?! Who's she with?!" The questions pounded at his head like a herd of stampeding cattle. The first thing he did was kneel down on his knees and pray. *"God help me I'm scared for my sister! Please protect her! Please God, give me peace of mind. Please."*

Almost instantly, Charlie felt a massive wave of relief and a supernatural sense of security wash over him. It was as if God himself was embracing him in a bear hug. Slowly but surely, he got to his feet and found himself knowing what the right thing to do was. "Thank you God." He murmured and went for his phone. He hated interrupting his parents time together, but he had no choice. Unless… maybe there was another way. Another idea entered his mind. Maybe he could get to Marcy. He had a blue quad he could try to find her with. He knew his parents wouldn't approve of him pulling such a stunt. In fact, his father was saving it for when he was fifteen because Charlie was not yet of legal age to drive a quad. But the fourteen year old cared about his sister too much to just sit back and do nothing. He just hoped Marcy wasn't too far away and even more so, he just hoped that she was okay.

…

Marcy however had no such qualms. She was just happy to be with Matthew and away from her overly-religious family. One of Matthew's friends, a twenty year old named Jerry Fifer, was speeding to Freedom at seventy miles per hour in his car: A bright orange 1957 Chevy Bel Air. Next to him was another friend of Matthew's: another Junior named Tyrone Carter. Her and Matthew were in the back, already cuddling. With the combination of Matthew's strong arms wrapped around her, and the wind whipping through her hair, Marcy Boxford had to admit that this was pure paradise.

"How have you been?" Matthew asked her loudly over the racket.

"Good. You?" Marcy replied.

"Great. Especially now that you're here." He replied and the duo kissed as they sped toward the park.

...

Meanwhile, Charlie was traveling around on his quad, nicknamed *Ferrari,* after his favorite type of sports car. He had a gut feeling Marcy would be at the park. It was where he had seen her hanging out with her non-Christian friends. He knew that's who she was with. Who else would she be hanging out with at night and away from their parent's watchful eyes? As the fourteen
year old got closer to the park, he just hoped that he was right so he could get his sister and go home before his parents realized what he was up to.

...

Meanwhile at the park, Marcy was still with Matthew and the rest of the kids. They were having a great time, but not a Godly time. Swear words and crude humor were thrown around like a dog chasing a ball and vapes and alcohol were being offered left and right. Satan was the king of this hangout. Matthew offered a vape to Marcy.

"Sorry Mattie, I can't do that." She said gently. This was the one thing she didn't like about Matthew. He was cool, cute, strong, honest, and funny, but he sometimes made foolish choices. This was one of those times.

"Why? Don't tell me it's because you're religious." He replied, the annoyance in his voice made very clear.

"My family is religious, not me." Marcy explained quietly. This was another reason why she hated having to be religious. There were too many rules! But even so, she didn't do drugs, vapes, or anything related. She knew the harmful effects and stayed away from them. But Matthew had often had trouble understanding Marcy's boundaries in the past, and unfortunately tonight seemed no different.

"If you aren't religious then what's the big deal?" He questioned.

"I just don't want to get sick."

"You won't get sick, you'll be fine."

"Mattie, sweetheart I just don't feel comfortable with it."

"Seriously?"

"Mattie, honey we've had this talk before. I need you to respect that." Marcy said as gently as possible.

Matthew just scowled. "I thought you knew how to have fun." The words stung Marcy like a giant wasp. Was Matthew losing interest in her?

"I do it's just-"

"Just do nothing but read the Bible." Matthew interrupted and stomped over to his friends. "Let's go." He said dryly and began to walk away with his friends.
"Wait! What about me?!" Marcy gasped.

"You can walk home." Matthew replied coldly.

Marcy ran forward and leaped into his arms. "Please! Don't leave me! I'm sorry I upset you!" "Go home Marcy. It's over." Matthew said, no emotion evident in his voice. "But-"

"Marcy don't make this any harder on yourself. It's for the best. And besides since me and Rachel have made up you're free to go.

Marcy's heart shattered into a million pieces. Her dream boy had been cheating on her the whole time! Matthew pushed her away and began to walk away when Marcy shoved him forward. Even though she wasn't as big as him, it almost made him fall over.

"Not bad. For a girl." He joked.

"I can do even better!" Marcy growled and took off her sweatshirt and threw it to the ground. She rolled up her sleeves and balled up her fists, willing herself not to wipe the tears away that were flying down her face. "I don't submit to any man!" She yelled.

The boys just laughed at her. "Good for you sweetheart. Now I'd recommend putting that sweatshirt back on because it's gonna be a long night for you." Matthew chuckled and walked towards his car. Marcy wanted nothing more than to charge him, but her feet would not do her bidding. Marcy watched in horror as the boys loaded into the Chevy, and drove away.

For two minutes that felt like two millenniums, Marcy just stood there, dumbfounded by what she had just experienced. Afterwards, her legs gave way, and she fell down and cried.

...

Marcy just sat on the chilly ground sobbing until she heard a motor. Had Matthew come back for her? No it wasn't a car motor. It was- *A Quad?* Marcy's heart leaped with hope as the motor drew closer. Suddenly, a pair of headlights showed and Charlie pulled into the park on his quad. He ran towards her and quickly helped her to her feet.

"Marcy are you okay? Did they hurt you?" Charlie asked her desperately. For a few moments Marcy was too shocked to respond. Charlie had come for her?

"Charlie...you're not...old enough..."

"I was worried about you!" He reasoned.
"You could get arrested!"

"So what?! You're my sister, I love you!"

Marcy was utterly shocked. Charlie had done nice things for her before but this was on a whole other level. "After what happened just this morning and what I said to you at church you-"

"Are forgiven." Charlie finished for her.

"How?" Marcy gasped, in awe of her brother's character.

"It's what Jesus would do, Marcy." Charlie

explained. "But what happened?" "He was...

with someone else...the whole time."

Adam embraced her in a big hug for a long time. "C'mon sis. Let's go home." Charlie said gently.

"Fine by me. But I'm driving." Marcy said sternly and took the driver's seat, much to her brother's disappointment. Charlie sat on the back as she drove them home. She only hoped they could both get home before their parents realized where they had been.

...

Marcy raced on to their home street and headed towards the house. *"Good thing there's no car in the driveway!"* She thought, relief flooding through.

"Alright we made it!" Shouted Charlie with joy. Just then, Marcy saw a black SUV round the corner. And it was heading straight for the house. Marcy gulped in fear as her parents pulled into the driveway.

...

Charlie expected Marcy to cheer with him but when she didn't,

he knew something was wrong. "Marcy...tell me I didn't just jinx

it." He said nervously.

"Yeah you little brat." Came her reply. "You jinxed it."

7

"What are you two doing?!" Their father screamed. It's almost 10:30 and you're out doing this?!"

"Is this disobeying your mother week or something?! In case you've forgotten, it's a school night!" Their mother hissed angrily.

"In the house now!" Their Father yelled in rage.

...

In the living room, the two kids sat down on the couch, their parents standing in the middle of the living room. Charlie was fidgeting his hands and Marcy was just sitting there, tapping her foot nervously. The room was deathly quiet.

"Well, who's going to come clean?" He boomed. "Where were you and what were you doing?"

Marcy sighed as she saw Charlie look at her, his eyes pleading her to explain everything for him.

"I...was hanging out with those kids again."

Her mother growled. "Why am I not surprised?"

"Why were you with them? I've told you before why I don't like them. So why were you with them?!" Her father demanded.

"This boy...Matthew Fenton...made me feel...very special and very loved." She explained shakily. It made her nauseous to even mention his name now, when before she had been sick with rage when her father criticized him.

"You should be feeling that here." Her father

growled in confusion and shock. "Well I don't."

Marcy retorted.

"And why is that?" Her mother questioned.

"With what happened recently...it's been...very hard."
"It's been hard for all of us. But this kind of rebellious behavior won't solve anything. At least tell us you can both see that now." The desperation in her father's voice was very clear.

"Yes." She and her brother said at the same time.

"Are you both ready to act more Christlike? Her father asked them.

"Yes." Charlie admitted.

"And what about you Marcy?" Her father asked her. Marcy's insides knotted with confusion and fear instantly. She hardly understood what Christlike meant. How was she supposed to act like that?

"I... don't know." She whispered. Her father nodded slowly and her mother rolled in eyes in annoyance.

"Well until you can figure that out you forget about having your car back." Her father stated seriously, the former desperation now gone.

"I can't figure it out! It's not that easy for me!" She yelled.

"And why is that? I'm the head pastor of your church, I've preached about being Christlike hundreds if not thousands of times!" He father exclaimed.

"And I never understand it!" Marcy yelled back.

"And why is that?" Her father questioned.

"You talk about things...scary things…that don't make sense to me."

"And why is that?" Her father asked.

"You tell me!" Marcy finally exploded. "You tell me why! Why would a God who loves everybody send people to hell just because they messed up?! And why would a God who's supposed to look after you and protect you, let bad things happen?! Do you know the kind of pressure that puts on me?!"

"Well since you're saved you shouldn't be worried about that! His ways are beyond ours Marcy. Bad things happen and only he knows why! It's hard for us sometimes not to be able to understand his ways, but we have to keep pushing forward and trust him. That's what faith in God is all about!" Her father explained in a loud voice.

Marcy just sighed. "Dad...I only went to the altar that night when I was ten because the stuff you constantly said was scaring me. I didn't want to go to hell! And I thought that if I accepted this God, you'd be proud of me, which you were! I didn't know what I was doing or saying, I was just trying to please my father!" She finally admitted. She had been holding these thoughts in for seven years. It felt good to finally be able to release them.

...

Charlie stared at his big sister in shock. *"So that's why she acts the way she does! She's never been saved at all!"* The thought broke his heart. But it all made sense now.

"Marcy...nobody here knew how you really felt. Why didn't you talk to us?" His father asked her as he sat next to her on the couch.

"I was scared you'd be angry at me." She whimpered and cuddled into him.

"I wouldn't have been angry at you sweetheart." Said their father and hugged her close. "Is that why you were with Matthew and the others and seeking attention from them? Were you scared of me?"

Marcy nodded. "I didn't want you to hate me because I don't believe in what you do."

Charlie's heart snapped in two for his sister. He could tell his parents felt the same way. His mother sat next to him on the couch and faced Marcy. "You know your brother has a fear issue." Marcy nodded. "And what does he do when he feels that way?"

"Talks to you about it."

"Exactly. So talk to us."

"Sometimes I feel like I can't talk to you guys."

"I know, but we're your parents. You can talk to us."

The children's mother reasoned. "I don't know." Said

Marcy.

"Why do you feel you can't talk to us?" Their father pressed.

"I don't want to be a burden to you guys after everything that's happened." Marcy whimpered. Charlie found himself trying to avoid crying. He knew where Marcy was going. And it was his fault that she felt this way.

"Honey, it's no burden." Their mother said.

"Me and your mother may have lost our parents but we love you even more than them. We don't want to lose you too. We couldn't." Charlie's father added.
"I know. And I'm sorry for the way I acted. Matthew didn't even love me." She whimpered through her tears.

"I'm glad you know you were wrong. I'm proud of you for that." Stated their father.

"You shouldn't be proud of me. It was my fault." Charlie said and began sobbing. His mother came over and gave him a big hug.

"It was not your fault." She said through her own tears.

"Yes it was! I told Marcy that all our grandparents should fly up and visit us. Marcy agreed and told you and Dad. And then, there was the pilot who died in mid-flight... and the plane...if I had just kept my big mouth shut they'd all still be here." He sobbed miserably.

"Son, you can't do that to yourself. You didn't know." Murmured his father.

"I know, I know. And it was part of God's plan. I don't understand his ways but I'm willing to trust him. His ways are perfect."

"I'm so proud of you that you know that." Said his father.

Marcy spoke up. "Charlie...how do you have

such faith? How do you get that?" "You don't.

God gives you it." Charlie explained to her,

wiping his eyes.

...

Marcy stared at her brother, wondering how he could be so confident in a God that had let his grandparents die. But as admirable as it was it almost...made sense?

"So you trust in God and he does the rest?" Marcy asked him slowly. She didn't know what she was getting herself into.

"That's right." Charlie nodded. Marcy thought deeply about something that she hadn't thought about for a long time. She'd obviously been rebellious against God for quite some time, constantly questioning if he really cared about her. But she had done quite a good job of messing up her life so far.

"Would he...still care about me?" She asked her family. Now that she knew her father cared about her, maybe the God he believed so strongly in felt the same way.

"Absolutely." Stated her mother.
"Certainly." Stated her brother.

"He'll always love you no matter what." Her father said with a confidence that seemed to empower him as he said it.

"Do you know how..."

"Repeat after me: Dear God, I know I'm a sinner and I'm sorry." Encouraged her father. Marcy repeated him. "I want to change." Marcy repeated him. "I'm willing to trust you with my life." March repeated him again and felt a power rising inside of her that she couldn't explain. But it felt good. "I'm ready to become a Christian." Marcy repeated him again and began to feel even better. "I accept you as Lord and Savior of my life." Marcy repeated him with a smile, a happy feeling inside her that she couldn't explain. Within mere and precious moments joyful hugs and kisses were being exchanged. Marcy Boxford had had a tough life, but things finally seemed to be going in the right direction. And with God by her and her family's side, what could go wrong?

...

The answer was soon to come. A mysterious man was on the phone with someone who had evil intentions for the household. And the crime they were about to commit would change the Boxford family and *Boxford Baptist Church* forever.

8

Charlie woke up for school on Monday. He had always loved school, especially science. His teachers thought very highly of him and he worked hard to please them. After getting dressed he raced downstairs to eat breakfast and found Marcy on the couch.

"What time did you get up?" He asked her.

"Twenty minutes ago." She replied.

"What were you doing?"

"Praying." Marcy answered with a smile. Charlie smiled back and the siblings quickly embraced each other. As they parted they got themselves some breakfast.

"What were you praying about?" Charlie asked as he prepared his waffle.

"Everything." Marcy replied as she prepared some toast. "My new faith. You. Mom. Dad. And...our grandparents." She finished slowly.

"They were saved Marcy. I know that for a fact." Charlie stated confidently. Marcy stared at him, confusion in her eyes as they sat down to eat their waffles.

"Now why can't you have that same confidence with your issue with Derrick?" She questioned him. Derrick Anderson was the captain of the school football team and thought Charlie was the biggest "science nerd" ever. And unfortunately, he didn't mind reminding Charlie what he thought about him either.

"It's not that easy." Charlie sighed as he chewed on his waffle.

"Yes it is. You're only missing one thing. You know what that is?"

"What?"

"Confidence. Have you ever heard of it?" She questioned playfully.

"I've heard of it, I'm just not good at putting into practice."

Charlie sighed miserably. "Well if you think you're beaten

you are." Marcy stated coldly as she sat down next to him.

"Marcy it's just-"

"Look I'm telling you the truth. I'm speaking from personal

experience too." "Yeah right." Charlie laughed. "It seems you've

never been scared about anything or of anyone."

"That's not true." Marcy stated to his surprise. "Did I ever tell you about Hailey Robertson?" Marcy asked him after she swallowed a bite of her waffle.

"No, I don't think so."

"She was my bully back when I was nine." Marcy said seriously. "And she used to scare me and try to hurt me. And eventually I grew to be mighty ashamed that I wasn't sticking up for myself against someone who was only an inch taller than me."

"So what'd you do?" Charlie asked, the new

story making him very curious. "I stood up

for myself."

"Was it hard?"

"Very hard. It took everything in me to keep myself from shaking. But I had had enough of being picked on so I got up and did something about it. I told her off and she backed down pretty quickly. After that, Dad taught me self defense and I've never had any issues with confidence ever since."

The story shocked Charlie. He nodded slowly and then smiled mischievously. "And then you use those cruel tactics on your innocent little brother." He quipped.

"You? Innocent? Now I've heard everything." Marcy joked.

"Hey I'm not that bad."

"You tried to kill me just yesterday."

"What? I did not!"

"Yes you did. You shot me!"

"When did I-oh. *Hammerhead.*" Charlie laughed at the memory.

"And for your information the bruise is still there!"
"Aww, did the invincible Marcy Catherine Boxford take a hit she can't handle?" Charlie teased her.

Marcy's mouth hung open in fake offense. "You little...I'm going to make sure you take some hits you can't handle when we get home!"

"Bring it." Charlie snarled playfully as he took another bite out of his waffle.

Marcy's eyes widened in surprise. "You're actually serious?" Asked Marcy after she swallowed a piece of her waffle.

"Yeah. Why not?"

"You never wanted to do anything like that before. What changed you?"

"Your story. If you can be brave, so can I." Charlie stated, surprised by the confidence in his voice.

"Then stand up to Derrick when he picks on you."

"And you're going to be right there with me, right?"

Marcy shook her head no. "You gotta stick up for yourself by yourself. If I stand up for you, you learn nothing."

Charlie sighed. He knew she was right. "Alright. I promise I'll try." He said as they both finished up their waffles.

"Good. Now get ready for school." Marcy told him.

"Yes Mom." Charlie mocked and they both laughed.

Before the kids left to catch the bus, they prayed for success on Charlie standing up to Derrick and that they would both use the story for God's glory.

...

Marcy's day was pretty normal, except for the part where she casted an angry and unfriendly glare at Matthew and his real girlfriend Kylie. The two mean kids just laughed and kept walking. It didn't bother Marcy though. So what if Matthew Fenton didn't love her? God did. And for Marcy Boxford, that was good enough for her.

...

Meanwhile, it was showdown time in the *Stamford High School* gym. Derrick was already stomping towards him. Charlie willed himself not to run.

"What's up nerd? Read any good books lately?" He asked mockingly.

"Lately no. But I built a catapult named *Hammerhead.*" Charlie replied, keeping his voice steady.

"How about I hammer your head?" Growled Derrick. By now a small crowd of kids had gathered to watch the fiasco.

"Yeah I don't think so. I would want to get hammered by someone who's actually cool." Charlie replied calmly.

Derrick stepped back, his brown eyes wild with shock. "Excuse me? You don't think I'm cool?"

"You used to be. But after you lost us the championship game last week when you fumbled the ball which let *Houston* win...well, I'll be honest with you, I've been having second thoughts a lot lately." Charlie explained slyly. The crowd of kids which had grown larger "oohed" and "aahed." Derrick went red with rage.

"How dare you?!" He shrieked.

"How dare you what?" Said Coach Carl from behind. "Charlie's right. Did I not tell you to practice your catching at home?"

"Yes." Mumbled Derrick.

"And did you?"

"No."

"And why is that? Do you remember? I know I do." Said Coach Carl seriously.

"I was hanging out with a girl." He whimpered. He knew his football coach was about to reveal his big secret.

"From what I heard from both her parents and yours that you did more than just "hang out" with the girl whose father just happened to catch the two of you." Derrick closed his eyes shut, obviously trying to pretend that none of this was happening right now.

"I...uhh..." He stammered.
"Also, me and Principal Ryan have wanted to speak to you about the way you treat some of our Honor Students. Charlie over there in particular. And now seems like a great time. So come along."

"Yes sir." Derrick mumbled miserably. And on the spot, a standing ovation was given to Charlie Boxford, the smart kid who wasn't afraid of anybody, even Derrick! Charlie exchanged high fives and fist bumps from everybody in the room. Marcy was one of them. She had come by to see Charlie and make sure he'd be okay. And he was. In fact, Charlie Boxford felt better then ever! Unfortunately for him and his sister, their great day was about to become the worst day of their lives.

9

On the bus ride home, everyone was talking and about Charlie's victory over Derrick. Even though was normally a great football player, it didn't take a genius to realize the young man had some major growing up to do. Marcy was the proudest of all of them.

"That's my brother!" She'd say whenever anybody else praised him. Charlie would just blush sheepishly and laugh along with them. It felt good to be liked.

"So this is what it's like to be popular!" The fourteen year old thought happily to himself. Unfortunately and unbeknownst to him and Marcy, their family was quite popular with other people as well, who unlike the kids on bus SO-4, weren't in favor of any of the Boxford's family accomplishments.

...

Bus SO-4 dropped the siblings off at their normal bus stop.

"Epic day today huh!" Marcy said proudly as they walked towards their street.

"Tell me about it!" Charlie squealed in delight. "I'd always imagined being popular, but I never imagined that it would feel this good!"

"I always tried to tell you but you were too scared to

do anything to prove yourself!" "Tell me about it! And

thanks for your help Marcy."

"Sure." She replied. There was a short silence until Marcy broke it. "Race you to the house!" She yelled and took off running, Charlie instantly in hot pursuit. They ran home and arrived at the same time, but what they saw made their stomachs turn upside down and gasp in horror.

Cop Cars were everywhere and the house was damaged. Several windows were broken and the front door had been shattered into a million pieces. On the see-through side porch, their mother's roses, violets, and other plants were toppled over and demolished. Marcy's car had had all its tires sliced and all the windows were smashed. The steering wheel had been shredded to pieces as well. Just then, an officer came running up to them.

"Hey kids, bad news. Your parents were

kidnapped." He explained solemnly. "What?!"

Charlie and Marcy shrieked at the same time.

"I'm so sorry. We'll find them. In the meantime, you'll be staying with somebody you know well." The moment the officer finished speaking, a dark blue Pontiac Vibe pulled up. The children recognized the car and the person that emerged from it. Ali Hussein ran towards them and embraced them.

"We'll find them. We'll find them." Ali kept murmuring quietly as Charlie and Marcy sobbed and hugged him.

...

A week later, the cops still couldn't find anything. The criminals are obviously experts and had covered their tracks well. Charlie, Marcy, and Ali constantly prayed for a miracle, but it didn't seem like hope was anywhere near the trio. Katie and her mother stopped by a few times and Charlie would often cuddle with Katie just like when he was much younger. Marcy used to make fun of him for it, but she didn't dare do that now. Anything that kept her brother out of despair, Marcy was for it. The older girl was glad she'd made up with her family before this horrible tragedy struck. She had apologized to Mrs. Scotts and told her and Katie about her turn to Christ. They had taken the news well and had encouraged her greatly. It felt great to have friends like Katie and Mrs. Scotts.

Katie's father had died of a heart attack when she was only eight years old. Katie could relate to the fear of not having a father and two often talked about their experiences and feelings. Katie encouraged Marcy to be patient and wait for God to work, but both her and Charlie were getting tired of waiting. Marcy could tell that Mr. Hussein felt the same way. He had served in Desert Storm and was constantly on his military computer. Marcy had always had a fascination with military equipment and could tell even by a quick glance that he was searching for her parents.

...

Another week passed and there was still no sign of Marcy's parents. Just when all hope seemed lost, Ali burst into the living room, a big smile posted on his face. "I found them! I found them!" He exclaimed cheerfully.

Marcy and Charlie were thrilled. "I'll tell the cops the good news!" Marcy stated happily and reached for her apple phone. But Ali reached out and stopped her.

"No, don't bother. They're in a place where cops won't be of much use."
"Where's that?" Charlie questioned.

"Iraq."

"What?!" Both the kids screamed.

"You heard me. Your parents are in Iraq in a town

called Saminga." Ali explained. "Saminga? Didn't you

help the Americans take over that town?" Charlie

questioned.

"Ahh, So you remember that story do you?" Ali said with a large smile. He had told Charlie and Marcy countless stories about his military career.

"Yeah that was shortly before your friend Ryan Hawking went to jail right?" Charlie asked.

Ali sighed deeply. "I still am still certain to this day that my Brother In Christ is innocent. I haven't been able to visit him lately. I do hope he is well."

Marcy spoke up. "I'm sure he is. God will always be with him."

Ali nodded in agreement. "What you say is true. And God is also obviously for me finding your parents."

"You mean us." Stated Marcy sternly.

"What?" Said Ali.

"They're our parents." Said Charlie standing beside his sister. "We're going to help find them."

Ali shook his head. "That's not going to happen. It's admirable what the two of you want to do, but you're both still kids. It'll be too dangerous for you."

"But they've done everything for us! Mr. Hussein, we can't just sit back and do nothing!" Charlie protested.

"You can't tell us no Mr. Hussein! We love our parents and
we're willing to do anything for them!" Marcy added.

Mr. Hussein scratched his chin and sighed. "I can see there's no
convincing you kids otherwise. I'll give you one warning and one
warning only: This will be an extremely difficult journey beyond
what you could possibly imagine. Once we hit the road, there's no
turning back. So if you're coming, you're in. But if you do, there's
no returning home. So which is it?"
It was nearly fifteen seconds before the kids responded. Marcy
looked at Charlie and the kids nodded in agreement. It was
officially decided. "We're in." Marcy told Ali, her eyes wild with
confidence. Charlie had the same look.

"Alright then. Pack your things. We leave tonight for the
airport." Hussein ordered. The kids quickly obeyed, shaking
with excitement. What an adventure this would be!

...

The last twenty years of Ryan Hawking's life had been anything
but an adventure. The only type of excitement the former soldier
ever experienced at Delaware State Prison was a daily prison
fight. Nevertheless, his faith in God remained the same. He had
brought three people to Christ so far and the change in their lives
had helped them get out of prison and move on with their lives
much quicker. Even better, Ryan had learned from his old friend
Ali Hussein that a friend from Ryan's high school, David Boxford,
had founded *Boxford Baptist Church* and brought countless souls
to the cross. He had a wife named Louise and two children
named Marcy and Charlie. The thoughts overjoyed him. Even
cooler, Ali was a Deacon there too! Ryan's heart swelled with
pride for his friend. Ali sure had come a long way! But even
though the news from Ali was great, Ryan couldn't help wishing
he was roaming free instead of being locked in cell 118 nearly
twenty four hours a day.

Suddenly, his cell door was opened and there stood a cop. There
were hundreds of cops at the prison but Ryan had never seen

this guy before. And there was something about him that was a little perculiur. Ryan just couldn't place his finger on what it was.

"Come with me Ryan Hawking. You're being released today." The man said gallantly and pulled Ryan to his feet. The ex-soldier didn't know how to respond.

"Right this way." Said the cop. Not knowing what else to do, Ryan did as he was told. The mysterious man led him through the corridor and into the main lobby. As the duo walked through the lobby, Ryan was shocked beyond belief that nobody, cops or anyone else, was acknowledging that their number one prisoner was escaping! They strode outside and over to an F-250 Pickup Truck.

"This...is yours?" Ryan asked slowly.

"No. It is yours." Replied the cop.

"Why...why are you helping me?" Ryan asked cautiously.

"I have a job for you." Stated the cop as a matter of factly and reached into his pocket and handed Ryan a plane ticket for a flight bound to...

"Iraq?" Ryan stated in surprise. "What do you want me to go there for?"
The cop smiled knowingly. "Two children and their parents

are in need of your assistance." "What-What can I do to help

them? I'm a criminal."

The cop pointed to the sky. "Not to him."

Ryan was surprised. "You're a believer?"

"Yes I am." The cop said with a chuckle.

"Why-how...I don't understand this." Ryan admitted.

The cop stared at him seriously. "You don't have to. God will direct you if you're willing to trust him. Are you willing to do that?"

"Yes. I am."

"Off you go then."

"Okay..." Ryan stammered and climbed in the truck, still unsure of what was happening. Was this a dream? He pinched himself and it hurt. Whatever this was, it was for real.

He turned to thank the mysterious cop for his help...but he was gone. Ryan got out of the truck and peeked around everywhere. But the cop had vanished without a trace.

Ryan got into the truck again, breathing heavily, now realizing what had just happened to him. He had just had an angelic encounter! God had sent his angel to deliver him from prison. But why? To help a random family in need?

Ryan took a deep breath and started the truck. He didn't understand why God wanted him to help these people, but he knew for sure that God's ways were higher than his, and more than often, unexplainable. And with those thoughts in mind, Ryan Elias Hawking started driving towards the airport, wondering what the family needed from him, and why he was being sent there. And through those thoughts he learned something else: God wasn't done with him.

10

"Are you both ready to go?" Called Mr. Hussein.

"Yes sir." The kids replied as they finished packing their things.

Just then, Marcy received a text from Katie:

"Hey u wanna hang out later and talk?"

Marcy wanted to tell Katie about her quest more than anyone, but Mr. Hussein had made it clear not to inform anybody about the mission they were about to undertake. *Sorry I'm busy helping Mr. Hussein today with stuff."* It wasn't a lie.

"Oh okay. Maybe another time."

"Sounds awesome to me." Marcy replied. But the seventeen year old girl couldn't help wondering if yesterday was the last time she would ever see Katie.

...

Charlie was having similar thoughts. His grandparents were devout Christians but even they didn't know the time that they would depart this world and head to the next. For that matter, nobody ever did. Only Father God himself knew the answer to such a deep and powerful question. He was still grieving not only his loss, but the feeling that he was still partly responsible for his grandparent's death. If only he hadn't talked to Marcy about having them come visit! He still remembered the conversation like it was yesterday:

"Hey Marcy, are you excited for Easter?" He had asked.

"Totally. And I can tell you are." Charlie remembered blushing at

his older sister's teasing quip. "Is it really that obvious?"

"You're so excited you sound like you're five."
"Well c'mon Marcy, it's Easter! Who wouldn't be?" Charlie

had stated almost indignantly. "I honestly can't name

anyone." Marcy had admitted.

It was then that he had spoken the sentence he had grown to despise himself for saying: "Hey, How about all our grandparents come down for Easter?"

"That's a good idea. We haven't gotten to see them for a while."

"Maybe you can talk to Mom and Dad about it. Since you're older they'll probably be more likely to listen to you."

"Alright Charlie, I will. But you need to get more self confidence."

"I don't know…"

"Look kiddo, I know it's hard to step up with your own ideas sometimes, but if you don't start now, it'll be all the harder in the future."

"Yeah, I know. I'll think of something."

Charlie sighed, wiping away a couple tears from his cheeks. If only he had kept his mouth shut! But he couldn't think that way. His grandparents would want him to move forward and to not let his grief overcome him. And so that's what he would do: move forward, no matter what the odds of success were.

...

The flight at the airport left for Iraq at 9:00PM. Ironically, Ali had them leave at 7:15PM. Why was Mr. Hussein leaving so early? After all, the airport was only half an hour away. Oh well, Charlie didn't care. The sooner he found his parents, if he did at all, the better. He had brought his homemade slingshot with him to remind of science, his best happy place.

The trio was traveling down Hudson Road and were making good time. The airport was only three minutes away now and Charlie could see it in the distance. Trees were everywhere along both sides of the road. As the trees passed by, Charlie kept picturing what kind of animals lived there. Physics wasn't his first science he was into. It was wildlife. Charlie still made sure his knowledge of the creatures God had created was up to date. It was fascinating the incredible things that God could come up with.

They rode in silence until a gunshot rang through the trees. The next sound was the explosion of the left front wheel. The third sound was the Pontiac Vibe screeching to a halt on the side of the road.
"Wha-what happened?!" Charlie shrieked.

"In the trees! Now!" Screamed Mr. Hussein. The trio shakily and quickly departed the now totaled Pontiac Vibe and raced toward the forest like a mouse trying to escape a cat. The difference was that this "cat", whoever he or she was, had a gun. But similar to a cat, it had its eyes on its prey and had the same intentions.

"Get to the airport! We'll be safer there than here! Yelled Mr. Hussein. As soon as he finished speaking, another shot rang out and shattered a small tree to smithereens no more than a foot away from him. Several more shots rang out in near missing unison, each one dangerously close to the three targets. Nevertheless, somehow by some kind of miracle, the kids and their adult counterpart made it safely to the airport. The place was already bustling with cops and other kinds of security guards, all on high alert. It wasn't surprising. The forest was so close there was no doubt that more than a few people had heard the gunshots. An extremely shaken up Marcy and Charlie sat down on the floor and cuddled with each other, their hearts pounding as hard as a massive stampede of Elephants. Mr. Hussein filled the cops in on everything. Remarkably, he was very calm. But then again, he was an ex-soldier of the United States. He had lived through these scenarios enough times that Charlie supposed he was used to the feeling.

"So you never got a good look at him?" A cop asked Mr. Hussein

"Unfortunately no. I don't even know if it was a man. All I knew was the person's intentions." Mr. Hussein replied gravely.

"Do you know why this person was after you three in such a way?"

"No, I don't. I wish I did. Marcy and Charlie are good kids. Not the kind to make enemies. And they got those traits from their parents. As for me, I was once in the armed army. But I was never of high command. And if somebody like a terrorist wanted revenge, he wouldn't have gone after me."

The officer nodded his head in agreement. "Well, I'm just glad you and the kids are safe sir." Said the cop thankfully.

"Oh forget about me. Marcy and Charlie are practically my own children as well. I'm best friends with their father. I couldn't lose them." Suddenly, the officer eye's went wide in recognition.

"Hey wait, those are the kids whose parents were

kidnapped!" Mr. Hussein nodded sadly. "Yes."

"You said you're going to Iraq with them?"
"Yes, it's where I'm from. I figured since they love to travel so much, it would help them to get their minds off it." Mr. Hussein

explained. Charlie looked up in surprise. He had never seen Mr. Hussein lie before. But under the circumstances, it made sense.

The officer smiled, believing the fib. "Well I hope you three have a much better time than you just did!"

Mr. Hussein laughed in agreement. "I'm sure we will! Thank you for your time! Good luck catching the physco."

"Thank you sir. We'll catch whoever it is." The officer replied as he walked away.

Mr. Hussein sat down next to Charlie and Marcy and sighed. "You kids okay?" Charlie And Marcy nodded in reply.

"You know...when you said we'd be facing a challenge unlike ever before...I didn't think that meant...getting shot at." Charlie mumbled.

Mr. Hussein patted him on the shoulder. "I know, I wasn't expecting it either. But God got us out of it, did he not?"

"Yes he did. Thank you God." Whispered Charlie happily.

"The cops told me that our flight will be delayed for

another hour." Said Mr. Hussein. "True but that won't

affect us. Good thing we left early." Charlie replied.

Marcy spoke up. "He shouldn't have missed us. There's

no doubt the guy was trained." "Maybe he had a bad

trainer." Charlie suggested.

"If so I'm glad he did." Marcy said.

"I guess I'll still have to put up with you huh?" Charlie joked.

"And unfortunately I guess I'll still have to put up with you!" Marcy retorted and pushed him gently. Even Mr. Hussein began laughing.

...

After that, the day went on as normal. Charlie, Marcy, And Mr. Hussein boarded their lane at 9:00PM, just as planned. What they didn't know was that another ex-soldier was on the plane. Ryan Hawking sat only a couple seats behind the trio, taking no notice of them or anybody else.
He was too busy praying that whatever God was planning, he would use him in a mighty way. And little did he know, his prayer would soon be answered.

...

Meanwhile, Marcy was having her own thoughts. *"How are we possibly still alive? Whoever was shooting at us had pretty good aim. No doubt they were well trained. And someone who's well trained can't miss like that! The trees couldn't have been much protection! We were sitting ducks! Why didn't the person just take us out?"* She wondered to herself. Those questions would also be answered. And the reason behind the attack would be all the more terrifying.

11

At 2:00PM the next day, the plane landed and Ryan Hawking got off the plane. He remembered this place well and had hoped to leave it behind. But God had called him here for a purpose, so Ryan was willing to trust him. By the end of the day, the middle aged man had checked into a hotel as if on any ordinary vacation. He then prayed that God would show him what to do next, unaware that a sinister figure was watching his every move.

...

Meanwhile, at an old castle in the mountains, a sinister plot was unfolding. And two lonely and worried parents were witnessing it in person. To their surprise, David and Louise Boxford weren't beaten or tortured. In fact, the married couple were treated like royalty. Fancy clothing and food were handed to them left and right. Even more strange, they were thought of as heroes. The people praised and thanked them as if they were angels as they seated them at a massive wooden table. The table was in a grand room that looked like something from the days of knights and castles. Despite such grand treatment, the couple knew that something strange was afoot, so they kept themselves on high alert at all times.

"David, sweetheart, what is all this?" Louise asked her husband

nervously. David sighed. "I don't know. But I do know this:

whatever is going on here certainly isn't Godly."

"Not Godly?!" Boomed a voice from behind. A man in a white suit emerged, red tie, and other fancy clothing strode onto the balcony that overlooked the kitchen, his eyes full of devotion and motivation unlike David and Louise had never seen. His bald head glistened brightly, shining like the sun. "At this place, we're all about the man upstairs!" He exclaimed loudly, looking somewhat offended.

"Then why do you treat us as though we're gods?" David questioned.
"Simple. You two are the ones who will help me be your country's salvation!" He exclaimed, a look in his eyes a proud father would have when his son learns how to ride a bike. David could relate to that feeling. But there was something ominous about this man that David didn't trust at all.

"Jesus Christ is everyone and every country's salvation! If you were a true Man Of God, you would know that!" Louise retorted bravely. David smiled in admiration of his wife's strong faith.

The mysterious man in the fancy clothing however, was not smiling. "I used to believe that. But it didn't work out so well. He let me down." He said solemnly.

"What happened?" David asked, genuinely concerned. A person who said things like that was nothing but hurt. Suffering was normal in a fallen world. But as a Christian and a Pastor, he knew full well that Jesus could take away any hurt, no matter how big. But too many people trusted in their own power to solve their problems. They didn't trust in God's unlimited power to bring them hope and freedom. And because of that, many people stopped seeking the Lord, and some outright refused him altogether. David had been a pastor long enough to know when someone was struggling in their faith. The mystery man seemed to be no exception.

"I… lost my entire family." The mystery man sighed.

"How'd that happened?" David pressed gently.

"My wife, my two daughters, my parents, and my younger brother were flying down from NY in 1980 to Florida to help me start a Baptist Church. But the pilot, who was a Christian as well, had a heart attack...and the plane went down. I lost everything. Your Jesus Christ failed me and my family! So I stopped believing in him! But if in some crazy way he is real, you and your family are going to help me make him pay!"

"We are sorry for your loss sir, but we're not helping you lead souls away from Christ!" David stated strongly.

"And we have our children to get back to! So let us go!" Louise put in.

The man just chuckled. "That's not going to

happen. I need you. Allah needs you." "Allah?!"

"Yes. After my loss I began studying different religions and gods. Jesus may have failed me but I knew the universe just wasn't born out of nothing. I settled eventually in the Muslim Faith. But I didn't want to make my new belief known just yet. So I settled on everyone thinking that I was an Atheist. And I lived my life quite well too. In 1988 I became the commander of the 75th Ranger Regiment until 1991. I helped America win a huge victory by taking over the town of Saminga in Desert Storm. That was my most notable achievement. But as time went on I realized something: Too many people, specifically Americans, still believed in Jesus Christ. It was, and still is, truly sickening that people weren't praising the right god. But I knew I couldn't convince them to just change their faith so I realized I'd have to force them to praise Allah. And shortly before my grand takeover or Saminga, I began planning the takeover of Christianity in the US."

"And if people don't submit to Allah? Then what?" David pressed.

The man just smiled. "That's why I have nukes. Ones I designed. I was in the US Army. I know what kind of nukes and other kinds of weaponry are difficult to track. I made sure that my nukes were perfectly designed to slip right by any US post, military base, or anything else."

"You'd destroy your own country?! The country you fought for?!" Hissed Louise in disbelief.

"Destroy is a rather strong word Mrs. Boxford. I like to think of it as...an improvement. It's the improvement the country needs!"

"Two things: One, you're insane. And two, how do me and my wife fit into all this?" David questioned.

"Oh Mr. Boxford I'm so glad you asked that! You see...I want Allah to be praised. Not Jesus. So who better to take the blame then a couple of Christians like yourselves?" The man said, pointing to David and Louise.

"What do you mean?" David scowled angrily.

"I mean that when the nukes are launched I'll make sure I remain innocent while you Christians take the blame!"

"Why would you do such a thing?" Louise growled.

"How else could I make your kind appear evil? How else could I convince people that Christians are physcos...and Allah has delivered the world from them. Countless people will join me in my quest to execute Christians and soon...Jesus and his followers will be reduced to nothing." He scowled. Louise and David were shocked beyond belief as he walked away. What an unspeakably evil man! To be in the presence of somebody so evil was truly terrifying. But David and Louise kept reminding themselves silently that ultimately, Mr. Psycho-Man was not in control. Jesus Christ was. And even if the evil plot somewhat succeeded, the couple knew for a fact that Jesus would not let his people be killed off.

...

Meanwhile, Charlie, Marcy, and Mr. Hussein had checked into a hotel and had prepared to go to bed after a long and scary day. "Mr. Hussein, how close are we to finding our parents?" Charlie asked him quietly.

"Oh we're close Charlie. In fact, I promise you'll see them tomorrow." Mr. Hussein replied confidently as he laid down in his bed

"That's a pretty big promise." Marcy said worriedly.

"Well I've got us this far, haven't I?" Mr. Hussein

questioned her with a chuckle. "Indeed. Thank

you." She replied.

"Well let's all get some shut-eye. We need it." Mr. Hussein said sleepily. After a quick prayer, the trio fell fast asleep.

...

For Marcy and Charlie however, it was hard to stay asleep. They were excited to see their parents. And Marcy's thoughts about the assassin were still buzzing through her mind like a hornet's nest. From across the room, she heard Charlie turn over.

"Hey Charlie, remember the psycho from earlier?"

"I try not to." He replied.

"I don't think he wanted to kill us."

"Go to sleep Marcy."

"Charlie, I'm serious."

"So am I. Go to sleep. And why would the person not aim to kill?"

"My theory is that he or she missed on purpose."

"What? Why would they do that?"

"I don't know. But whoever was shooting at us was well trained. They could have easily killed us on the spot." Marcy explained. Charlie's silence let Marcy know that she'd gotten through to him.

"I hope you're wrong." He murmured.

"I hope I am too." She replied softly.
"Can we stop talking about your conspiracy theories and go to sleep now?" Charlie groaned with a laugh.

"Yeah sure. Night. Love you." Marcy chuckled.

"You too." Charlie yawned in reply. And before they knew it, both siblings were finally able to get to sleep.

...

But what the duo didn't know is that Ali had heard everything. He too anticipated for tomorrow. It would be a day of deliverance. He thought about what Marcy had said. *"Smart girl. Too bad she'll never get to use that knowledge."* He chuckled to himself.

12

Just a few miles east of the children and Ali, Ryan Hawking awoke in his hotel. He peeked outside. The sun was shining bright and there was not a cloud in the sky over the town of Saminga. Ryan remembered this place well. The bloodshed and violence still sometimes haunted his dreams. But he had a job to do and he wouldn't be deterred. But how would he find the family he was supposed to help? He didn't even know their name! But he knew God would show him some kind of sign.

Suddenly, Ryan heard a *ticking* sound he recognized well. *"A bomb!"* He thought with great alarm. The ticking grew quicker and quicker and louder and louder. Ryan desperately searched for a way of escape. He couldn't jump out the window. It was too high. Ryan's heart began pounding. *"God help me! You couldn't have brought me all this way for nothing!"* He begged frantically in prayer.

Then...BOOM! A massive explosion sounded from below and the floor beneath Ryan gave way. The ex-soldier fell to the floor and hit the ground. Ryan Hawking's world went black.

...

"Good. Ryan Hawking is dead." The evil figure thought happily to himself. One thing that was puzzling is how the man made it out of prison and came this far? Oh well. Even if he had known what his boss was planning, there was nothing he could do about it now, that was for certain! *"Evans will still want to know about this though. He'll be happy that Ryan Hawking has perished. And I might even be rewarded!"* He thought happily to himself and quickly dialed a number on his phone.

...

In the deepest part of the castle, the evil man in the white suit and red tie was catching up on some sleep when the ringing of his big, black phone jolted him awake.
"This had better be good Mr. Arnold!" He growled to himself as he got up from his large, brown, leather chair.

"What is it?! It had better be some good news! I was taking a nap!" He scowled irritably.

"My sincerest apologies sir. But I thought you'd like to be informed of something very important and intriguing!" The voice on the other end of the phone stammered wildly.

"We'll spit it out then! I haven't got all day!" Growled the evil man in utter annoyance. *"This is what I get for hiring a nineteen year old nobody from the dirty streets of Los Angeles!"* He thought angrily to himself. From what he knew, Arnold Hutchinson had been a very troubled teenager and had had countless problems with his parents, teachers, and pretty much everybody. His parents had hated the sight of him and Arnold had finally had enough and had run off at age seventeen. The story had made the newspaper and the evil man needed an extra assassin. So one of his agents had told him about a brand new job opportunity. The young man easily had enough hate inside him to take up the role and the evil man himself taught him how to shoot. So far, the young man had done his job well. The evil man liked his skill, but not his mouth. He would never shut up and would use all these big and unnecessary words!

"You won't believe who I just killed!"

"Arnold please just tell me what happened. Who did you kill?" Whimpered the evil man as he sipped some of his juice.

"Ryan Hawking!"

The evil man spit his juice everywhere and began coughing

upa storm in bewilderment. *"Sir, are you alright? You don't sound so good."* Said Arnold worriedly from over the phone.

"I-I'm fine." He growled angrily. He hated people feeling

sorry for him.

"Are you sure? I mean, those coughs sounded pretty bad and-"

"I am perfectly fine Arnold and in no need of your sympathy!" Screamed the evil man into the phone. He then took a deep breath. "Now...tell me about...my friend." He said casually.

...

As Arnold relayed the events of Ryan's death to the evil man, Ryan Hawking came to. He couldn't believe it! God had delivered him again! Even more amazing, there wasn't a scratch on him! *"I wonder if this is how Shadrach, Meshach, and Abednego felt after their supernatural rescue by God in the furnace!"* He thought happily to himself.
Suddenly, he heard a voice on the phone outside, cheekily describing how he had killed Ryan Hawking. *"Well, life is full of disappointments."* Ryan thought as he creeped up behind the man. He ambushed him and the duo fell down a steep hill. The phone was crushed to dust on the way down.

...

Inside the castle, the evil man lost connection with Arnold. What had happened? Something was wrong.

And the evil man was right. Ryan and the assassin fell down the hill and into a large dump. Ryan's attacker pulled out a pistol and began shooting at him. Ryan ducked for cover behind an old car. *Pow! Pow!* Bullets whizzed by at astounding speed. Ryan pulled out his own pistol and returned fire. However, in a dump this big, there was plenty of debri to hide behind, and the mystery man quickly hid behind another abandoned car. *Pew! Pow!* Bullets were fired galore, but neither man could land a blow. Ryan realized his attacker's talent with a pistol was equal to his. Ryan knew he was running out of shots. His opponent most likely as well. So Ryan waited several moments until the firing from the other man stopped, then he fired. With no weapon to fire back with, Ryan's opponent was done for. In a matter of seconds, Ryan's opponent was shot down.

Ryan cautiously walked towards him. *"In war you never trust the enemy. No matter what."* Ryan thought. It had been his father's saying. But Ryan soon found the man was truly dead. He searched him for any ID of where he came from or anything useful but found nothing. He turned around...only to be staring into the muzzle of a rifle. WHACK! He was knocked unconscious.

...

Inside the castle, the Boxford couple longed for home.

"Louise, we have to get out of here. We cannot be a part of this man's evil plot."

"David look around you! There are three snipers in this room! And who knows how many more there are! We're trapped!"

David sighed. "You're right. But even so, we cannot support

something this evil and Ungodly." "I agree but you know they'll

kill us if we don't!" Louise hissed.

"Well, we're both saved so even if it comes to that, we're covered."

"It's not us I'm worried for David! I'm worried for our children!"

"They're saved too."

"Marcy just got saved! She needs us there to lead her more than ever!"

"I know how you feel Louise. I feel the same way. But we mustn't lose hope. God's on our side!" "I'm glad he is and I sure hope he works a miracle!"

"Me too. But until he acts let's think of anything else besides being here." David encouraged her. Louise nodded. "Okay. I remember...Charlie working on *Hammerhead*."

"Our son's powerful knowledge of science is truly amazing. And I remember Marcy with her vast knowledge of military equipment too."

"Yes I remember her and Ali chatting about military vehicles and the arrest of Ryan Hawking."

"You think he's holding up alright?" Asked David. "It's terrible being imprisoned for a crime you didn't commit."

"I sure hope-" Louise hadn't finished her sentence when David's question was answered. Two soldiers appeared and they dragged a struggling, middle-aged man into the room.

"What is the meaning of this?!" Boomed the evil man in fancy clothing who had come out of nowhere. But his eyes then went wide when he saw who his soldiers had brought him.

"Ryan Elias Hawking!" He gawked in astonishment.

David and Louise exchanged a shocked look.

...

Ryan gazed up at the man who had addressed him. When he saw who it was, his stomach flipped like a pancake being flipped in a frying pan.

"Commander Evans!" He gasped.

13

"Wha-wha-"

"Take your time old friend." Chris Evans interrupted elegantly. I imagine this must be quite the shock."

"That's the understate of the millennium sir! You're supposed to

be dead!" Ryan hissed in reply. "Key word: Supposed." Evans

retorted nonchalantly.

"Well if you haven't been dead, then why didn't you tell anybody? Do you realize I've been in prison for thirty years for the murder of...well...you?!" Ryan yelled.

"I faked my death. Somebody had to be the fall guy. And your offensive preaching made you an easy pick."

Ryan was astounded! "Why would you fake your death?!" He hissed. Ryan had always known he was innocent of the crime, but the new and insane revelation had just put everything on a whole other level.

Commander Evans stomped towards him, his eyes full of a hatred that was most obviously demonically influenced. "Forgive me for answering a question...with a question, but do you know why I took so much offense to your preaching Ryan?"

Ryan prepared to answer but his former commander held up a hand. "Never mind. I'll answer it for you. The reason is quite simple actually: I used to believe what you're still foolish enough to believe in. That was until the day when my entire family was killed in a plane crash. Jesus failed to save them and so therefore he failed me! So I turned to a different religion: The Musilum Faith. Allah opened my eyes and showed me the truth: That Christians are evil and that they must perish!"

"I thought you were an Atheist." Ryan said.
"I let everybody believe that I was. But shortly before we took Saminga, I began to put my true plan into action. Do you see those two people over there?" He asked Ryan. Ryan hadn't even noticed two people sitting at a big table until now.

"I sent a spy into the US to get me a pastor."

"Why would you need a pastor."

"To take the blame when I launch nukes at America."

"What?!" Ryan shrieked in horror. "You'd destroy the country you fought for?"

Commander Evans just laughed and looked at the woman sitting at the table. "Now that question sounds familiar! I'll give you the same answer Ryan: I consider destroy to be a rather strong word. I like to think of it as an improvement."

"So improving your country is blowing it to bits. Makes sense." Ryan reasoned.

"America is strong and will be able to rebuild. In the meantime, I'll have that Pastor and his wife take the blame for the launch and when the world sees what monsters Christians really are, I'll be able to convince them to praise Allah forever! Even better, millions of people will join me in my quest to execute Christians! And soon, the only thing that will be left of Christianity, is a giant pool of blood."

"You're sick." Ryan said.

"Call it what you want Ryan Hawking. I consider my plan the improvement the world so desperately is in need of." Evans boomed. He then turned to the soldiers who had been holding Ryan. "Take him away."

...

David and Louise watched in horror as Ryan Hawking was led away to some unknown location. Commander Evans turned to the guards standing closet to them. "Bring them too. I want these miserable and pathetic Evangelicals out of my sight!" He growled. The guards quickly did as instructed and David and Louise Boxford prayed harder than ever for a miracle.

...

Meanwhile, Mr. Hussein had recently left to get a Jeep for him and the kids to travel in. Charlie and Marcy were getting their belongings packed up. Charlie grabbed his slingshot and packed several small stones in his pocket. What good would they be? Charlie didn't know, but it would be fun to pretend he was David fighting Goliath. He stuffed his slingshot into his backpack and
turned around. It was then when he noticed a note sticking out of Mr. Hussein's backpack. He pulled it out and read its contents:

"Oh great Allah, your time is near. I look forward to exacting vengeance on the ones who have defiled your holy name. May the great Allah be praised and let the followers of Jesus Christ perish!"

Charlie began shaking and he sank to his knees. Marcy rushed over to him.

"Charlie what's wrong?" She asked nervously. Too horrified to even speak, Charlie handed her the note with a trembling hand. After viewing it, Marcy joined him on the floor and the duo wept bitterly.

...

Once they got control of themselves, they sat in silence for several more minutes, taking it all in. Mr. Hussein, they're greatest ally, had lied to them. And not just about finding their parents. About everything. Caring about them. Caring about church. Caring about salvation. Even caring about Jesus Christ and the Bible. It was all one massive lie. A horrid, evil, tragic, despicable lie.

Charlie rummaged through the backpack and found a map. The map showed a castle hidden in the mountains. There was a giant red circle around the castle. Charlie knew that's where his parents were.

"We have to get there." Charlie murmerd.

"Yeah, but how?" Marcy questioned.

The answer came from a rumble outside. Mr. Hussein had come back with the Jeep. Charlie peered outside. Mr. Hussein was walking into their hotel.

"He's coming! We need to leave now!" Charlie said. Marcy ignored him and reached into Mr. Hussein's backpack and pulled out his phone. She jabbed it onto a loose nail sticking up from the floor.

"True. But we don't want him communicating with whoever

he's working with." She reasoned. Suddenly, Charlie had a

cheeky idea. He grabbed a pen and paper and wrote his own

letter: **"Thanks for the ride, psycho. For your sake, I hope

Allah gives you another."** He taped the note on the door.

Marcy gawked at him. "You're crazy." She whispered. "It took you seventeen years to figure that out? That says a lot." Adam

replied.

The two kids finished getting their stuff together, when Mr. Hussein came into the room. It took everything the duo had to keep from shaking. Charlie prayed his former friend didn't see the note or the phone until they were gone.

"Got everything ready kids?"

"Yeah, we'll take our stuff down now." Charlie said quickly and the kids barged past him and shut the door quickly. The enraged scream they heard behind them made them quicken their pace. They made it to the Jeep and jumped in. Marcy took the wheel. Normally, Charlie would have objected, but considering the current situation, Charlie didn't feel that was a good idea. As Marcy drove off, Mr. Hussein leaped on the back and managed to get on the roof. Marcy hit the brakes hard and the evil man was sent flying into front of them. Marcy raced forward but Mr. Hussein managed to roll out of the way in time. Though they had lost him for now, the shouts from behind them told them she was far from finished.

...

Back in America, Ryan Hawking's photo was everywhere. The news told about his escape from prison at least three times per day.

...

At a secret US military base located in Madagascar, a commander by the name of Max Barkley had been tracking Ryan Hawking since day one. Now he was sure he had him. The man was located in Iraq, Saminga to be exact.

"They really do always return to the scene of the crime." He thought to himself. Well, it was over for Ryan Hawking, that was

for sure. Max Barkley quickly got a strike team together and headed for Iraq.

14

"Nooooo!" Screamed Ali in a hateful, demonic rage. Those little brats had found him out! How dare they stand in the way of the great Allah's coming! His boss would not be pleased. Ali didn't want to upset him. Not for fear of getting punished, but for letting him down after all he had done for him.

As he ran back to Saminga to get another Jeep, he thought back on his life. His father had had many wives and he had treated them all horribly. Ali had watched Mohed Hussein kill his mother when he was just ten years old. He had initially been terrified and horrified by his father's despicable action and had run away from home. But Saddum had found him and had explained his reason behind his act. Ali remembered the conversation well:

It had been a dark and cold night. Rain had been pouring like cats and dogs. Ali was trapped in an alley, his father standing in front of the only exit. His father matched his forward. Young Ali screamed in terror and tried to climb the fence. But to no avail. He was too small and because of the rain, the fence had been too slippery. He fell backwards and his father caught him and set him down.

"Stay away from me!" Ali had yelped.

"I understand my boy. You just witnessed a horrible thing. I don't blame you for how you feel." His father had replied, the rain running down his face.

"You killed mom! You killed her!" Ali had screeched in Arabic.

"I know. But for a good reason." His father had

reasoned in the same language. "There's no

good reason to kill someone's mom, Papa!"

"Oh but there is."
"No there isn't Papa! There's no excuse for murder!"

"My dear son, there is one." His father had replied calmly.

"There-there is?" Ali had whimpered.

"Yes. We praise Allah right?"

"Yes Papa, we do."

"Do you remember why we hate Christians?"

"Yes. They follow the enemy of Allah."

Ali remembered his father nodding in approval. "That's right. And do you remember what we must to Christians, the enemy of Allah?"

"We must kill them Papa!" Ali had said strongly, his young and sweet voice already full of a demonic passion.

"That's right."

"But mother was no Christian Papa. She always gave her praises to Allah and to Allah only!" Ali had said.

His father had hung his head sadly. "There was a Christian who deceived her son. He poisoned her mind and she turned against Allah. So I was forced… to do the unthinkable…and kill her." He had sated softly, deep sorrow in his voice.

"Papa, does that mean she's..." Young Ali's voice had trailed off and he began breathing rapidly, thinking it couldn't be true.

"Yes my son. She's...not where she would have been." His father had stated.

Ali had screamed in emotional agony and leaped into his father's arms, sobbing uncontrollably. His father had done the same. They didn't even bother to come back home until the next morning.

...

Ever since that fateful night, Ali Hussein had had an immense hatred for Christians and for the god they followed. The grief and anger boiling inside his soul only got worse when his father died from a broken heart a week later. Ever since then, Ali had been his own. He had survived
as a street rat until Desert Storm broke out. He had been forced to abandon the secret hut he had built for a home thanks to the American troops burning it down. Ali had managed to escape in time but food himself scrounging around for food in the forest. That is until an American Corporal by the name of Ryan Hawking had found him trespassing on soil the Americans had recently conquered. Ali had expected to be shot on the spot, but instead Ryan had taken him to the base and introduced him to his commander, Christopher Evans. Ali remembered that conversation well too:

"Who is this Corporal Hawking?" Chris Evans had asked Ryan Hawking, eyeing Ali suspiciously.

"His name is Ali Hussein sir. I found him alone in the forest and brought him back with my squarderon. He poses no threat."

"Well it's a good thing he's not a threat. We already have enough of those." Evans had sighed.

"So what are we doing with him sir? He may be useful to us. He speaks very good English." Ryan Hawking had said.

"Is that so? Let's see it." Said the commander coldly.

"I am thankful...to be alive." Ali had said slowly. His father had taught him English and Spanish when he was little. When he had passed, Ali had continued the studies. And in this case, they had played out very well for him. All that studying sure had paid off!

Commander Evans had nodded slowly, satisfied with Ali's fluent English. "Very well then. You're dismissed Corporal. As for our new friend here, I'd like to talk with him in private."

"As you wish sir." Ryan had replied. As he opened the door, he turned to Ali. "May Jesus bless you Mr. Hussein and have a good day."

"I had just given you a direct order to leave! So

obey...Corporal!" Evans had growled. Ryan had given

Evans an annoyed look. "Yes sir." He had scowled and

closed the door.

"Christians." Ali had heard Evans mutter angrily to himself as Ali took the chair in front of his desk. Ali had been surprised and intrigued by the comment.

"I deeply understand and share your frustration sir." He had said emphatically.

Evans had leaned in close to him and had lowered his voice to a whisper. "Between you and me...I wish they were extinct." Ali's dark heart had leaped with joy. Now this was his kind of person! Somebody who's heart and mind were so dedicated to the destruction of Christianity that they loathed every Christian there was. "I blame them for the destruction of my family."

"Why is that?" Evans had inquired.

"My mother turned to their belief and my father had no choice but to. Kill her for doing so. He died of heartbreak a week later." Ali had explained in the same whispering voice that was full of pure malice. "I'd wipe every Christian off the face of the earth if I had the ability!"

Evans had leaned in even closer and had shared his own story: "I have the same emotions. You know why? I used to be foolish enough to believe their lies. But when I lost my family in a plane crash, I realized the truth: That Jesus Christ is dead."

"I'm glad you know that sir. But too many people still believe in their God." Ali had replied.

"You said if you had the ability to wipe out all the Christians you would. You see, I want Allah to be praised as badly as you do. What if I told you I could get you that ability and help you do so? What if I told you that I turn people to him and away from Jesus?"

Ali had been thrilled at the comment. "I'd love

that! But there's one problem." "What's that?"

"Your country."

Evans had nodded understandingly. "Too many Christians. I'm aware. But that's why I have several nukes being prepared by others like yourself who have already joined up with me."

"You'd destroyed your own country?!" Ali hissed in shock.

"Destroy is a rather strong word Ali. I like to think of it as an improvement. America is strong. It can rebuild itself."

"You wouldn't get away with it sir." Ali had reasoned.

"Oh but I would. See, I've been planning for this for almost a decade. And I know you're asking how I'd get away with such a deed. That's where you come in."

"Me?"

"Yes. You. As we've been talking I've realized

you're the perfect man for the job." "For what job?"

Evans had sat back in his chair and folded his hands on his desk. "Christians are evil but people don't believe that. So we need to make them look evil. That's where you come in. You'll go to America and find a pastor. You'll bring him to me and when I fire the nukes….guess who I'll make sure takes the blame?"

Ali had beamed. "Sir it's brilliant! I'm in!"

"Good. But let's get one thing clear. I'm in charge of this operation. You are not. Do I make myself clear?"

"Sir that's fine with me. I don't care who's in charge just as long as Allah gets the glory he deserves."

Evans had nodded in agreement. "And he shall. But beware. Christians are crafty. Sneaky. So get close to Ryan Hawking and pretend to convert to his faith at some point. I want you to learn their personality even better. Once he believes you're converted or shortly before , help me fake my death."

"Why would you want to fake your death?" Ali had asked.

"I've already demoted Ryan for preaching to me. When I'm "killed", everyone will believe he did it out of revenge. Once he's executed or put in prison, America will already hate Christians. And when the pastor you bring to me is blamed for the nuke launch, millions will join us in our quest
to execute Christians worldwide. And after all the dust settles, I'll have the power to convince the world to follow Allah!"
Evans had explained.

Ali had smiled a wicked smile and shook Evans' hand firmly. "I look forward to working with you." He had said. And at that moment, the ultimate trap for Christianity was under way. It had been decided then and there that it was time to put Christianity under siege.

...

But all the careful planning was close to being ruined. By American soldiers? No. By even adults? No. By the trickery of two children! In his rage, Ali hailed a car and tossed out the driver. He climbed into it and sped towards the mountains. Marcy's and Charlie's tricks were impressive, and they were good kids too, but like all good things, it as time for them and their parents to come to an end.

Steven Campagna

15

Marcy was driving at nearly 100 miles per hour across the desert.

"Aren't we going a little fast?" Charlie asked her.

"Nope. Not if we want to save Mom and Dad."

"But what can we do? Marcy we're just kids and who know how many people are working with Mr. Hussein?" Reasoned Charlie.

"I don't know. But we'll think of something." She replied.

"That is if we're not shot dead first." Marcy thought to herself. Whether she liked to admit or not, her brother was right. How could two teenagers fight against and withstand whatever and whoever was ahead. There was no way that Mr. Hussein was the only person involved in their parent's kidnapping.

"I want you to know something before we die." Charlie said.

"Charlie we're not-"

"You're the best sister ever."

"Charlie don't get all mushy!" Marcy hissed. Why did Charlie have to act like this? He always seemed to do this at the worst moments too. But after a few seconds of silence she realized she couldn't help herself either.

"Charlie we are not going to die! But if we do, I want you to know something...that you're the best brother ever."

Suddenly Charlie began laughing and pointing at her.

"What?!"

"You've told me countless times you don't have that big of a soft spot for me. But judging by your words, I admit I'm quite prone to disagree!" He chuckled.

Marcy growled as she blushed in embarrassment. "You little...I'd knock your block off if I wasn't driving you do know that right?" She yelled.

"Yeah I know. That's why I chose this specific time." Charlie retorted playfully and began laughing again. Marcy just shook her head in annoyance. As much as she wanted to pull over and smack him, she knew that getting to her parents mattered much more. Besides, if by some miracle they actually survived the impossible odds they were about to face, she'd have plenty of time to get Charlie back once they got home.

"You're trying not to laugh too." Charlie teased.

"No I'm-" Marcy couldn't even finish her sentence before

she broke down laughing herself. "Awww so you do love

me." Charlie snickered.

"Shut up."

"The truth's already out Marcy. There's no taking it back!"

"Yeah, whatever. Sometimes I lie."

"Maybe so. But I could tell you definitely weren't

lying about what you just said!" "Even so, don't

look too much into it."

"You know, lying is sin Marcy. You shouldn't lie. Especially if you're lying to the coolest and best brother of all time."

"Shut it Charlie."

"It's still a sin. There's no way around it." Charlie teased with a wink.

"Well, I've only been saved for a couple days kiddo! Cut me a break would you?" Marcy retorted playfully.

"Yeah I know. But I'm glad you are." Charlie said, all silliness gone from his voice."
"Yeah. Me too." Marcy replied in the same tone of voice.

The siblings rode in silence until Charlie spotted something. "Look! The castle from Mr. Hussein's map!" He said.

"Mom and Dad." Marcy whispered. She had

no doubt her parents were here. ...

Luckily, there were stairs from the bottom of the mountain that led up to the castle. Though the siblings reached the door without any problem, Marcy couldn't help feeling as though they were being watched.

"Do we knock?" Charlie asked her.

Marcy slapped her forehead in frustration. "This is warfare Charlie! You don't knock when you're at war!" She exclaimed.

"But it's the polite thing to do!" Charlie protested.

Marcy just sighed. Charlie had said some stupid things before, but this was on a whole other level! "Please stop talking. Your stupidity gives me migraines." She groaned irritably.

"Well then Miss I-Know-Everything, how are we getting in?"

"I'll think of something just give me a minute." Marcy hissed. She thought and thought then reached out and knocked on the door. It opened automatically, almost as if Satan was inviting them to Hell or some unforeseen nightmare.

Marcy walked in, Charlie close behind. They walked down a narrow hallway which was lit up with torches. Charlie started chuckling.

"You knocked."

"What? No i…" Marcy's voice trailed off.

"You knocked." Charlie repeated.

"Just shut up."

"You knocked." He said again.
"Shut up they'll hear you!" Marcy hissed. Finally, Charlie stopped yapping. The siblings eventually reached a large room with a large wooden table in the middle.

"What now?" Charlie asked. As if to answer his question, guards came out of nowhere and quickly grabbed hold of them. The teens struggled bravely, but were no match for men with military training.

"Stay still or die!" The man holding Marcy growled.

"Enough!" Called a voice from above. A bald man in fancy clothes came out of the shadows and stood on a balcony that overlooked the room.

"Sir we have two intruders!" Explained the man holding Charlie.

"They are not intruders! They are guests! And they will be treated as such! Release them this instant!" He yelled at them. The men quickly obeyed.

Marcy was grateful for the man's assistance but there was something about him that she still didn't trust.

The mysterious man rushed down and greeted them warmly.

"I apologize for the rough treatment. My men are very protective of me."

"It's...fine. Who-who are you?" Marcy asked nervously.

"Allow me to introduce myself: I am Commander Chris Evans."

"Commander...Wait a minute! You're supposed to be dead! You were assassinated shortly after you took over Saminga!" Marcy exclaimed. She had read books on the lives of some of the greatest military commanders and she knew for a fact that Chris Evans was indeed supposed to be dead.

"Key word Marcy Boxford: Supposed." He

said, looking somewhat offended. "You know

me?"

"And your brother. Hi Charlie."

"Uhhh...hi." Charlie said nervously.

"How do you know us?"

"I've been expecting the two of you, as have your parents."
"You know our parents?!" Marcy shrieked.

"Of course! Follow me, I'll take you to them!" He said happily. Marcy and Charlie quickly followed him down a long and old brick staircase, which led to something that looked like a dungeon.

And there, sitting gloomily in the cell closest to her, were her parents. Marcy and Charlie rushed forward to greet them. Their parents were overjoyed to see them but the joyous reunion was cut short when the same two guards as before grabbed them again. Marcy and Charlie struggled but were quickly tossed into the cell with their parents.

"Hey, what gives?" Charlie yelled. "We never did anything to you guys!"

"I know you and your sister must have a billion questions. But the man in the cell next to you can answer all of them for me. I'm too busy to be waddling around with you Christians." Commander Evans sneered and stomped off, his two guards following close behind him.

...

Marcy was shocked to learn that the man in the other cell was none other than the infamous Ryan Hawking. Even more astonishing and devastating was the story told to them by him and her parents. The utterly evil plot of Commander Evans was truly something truly abominable.

Marcy and Charlie filled the adults in on everything they had been through too. Mr. Hussein's betrayal shocked everyone, especially her father.

"So Ali Hussein has been bad all this time?!" Her father gasped in horror. Marcy was about to respond when a familiar voice sounded in front of the cells.

"Say my name and I magically appear!" Said Mr. Hussein gallantly. Beside him stood Commander Evans. Behind the sinister duo were a boatload of soldiers, Marcy estimated at least one hundred at bare minimum.

Commander Evans stepped forward and pointed a pistol at Marcy and her family. Ali pointed his pistol at Ryan Hawking.

"Thank you for your assistance in destroying Christianity. I'll ensure you'll all be well remembered." Commander Evans said with a sneer.

"Our God will stop you, you filth!" Marcy's mother hissed. Marcy marveled at her bravery. For so long Marcy had thought her mom had grown weak, but now she saw that the strong woman she once knew had always been there.
"Famous last words." Commander Evans replied and cocked his pistol. Mr. Hussein did the same.

Marcy dipped her head in sorrow. *"So this is how we go out."* She thought sadly. It was the end for the Boxford family.

16

Or so it seemed. Out of nowhere, massive explosions sounded from right outside. *Boom! Boom!* The ground shook violently.

"What's happening?!" Charlie thought to himself. He looked over and saw Commander Evans and Mr. Hussein panicking too.

"What is this?" Mr. Hussein panicked.

"Nothing good." Replied Commander Evans and turned to his troops. "Go and repel the attack! Do what you must! We didn't come this far to be stopped!" He howled in rage. His troops raced up the stairs alongside Mr. Hussein. Commander Evans scowled at Charlie's father, pure malice across his furious face.

"What have you done, pastor?! What sort of trick have you pulled?!"

"Beats me, but I'll happily take it!" He replied with a smile.

"Same here!" Charlie's mother piped up. "I have no idea what's going on but it sure seems like an act of God!" She quipped.

Commander Evans just growled and ran upstairs to command his troops against the unknown threat.

...

Little did she know, Louise was right. It was an act of God! But what she also didn't know was who the attackers were. They were the American Troops led by Commander Max Barkley.

"Storm the castle! Press the attack! But bring back Ryan Hawking! I want that man alive!" Yelled Barkley into his headset from inside his tank. He'd waited for this moment a long time. He finally had Ryan Hawking right where he wanted him!

...

Inside the dungeon, another explosion shook the room. Bricks fell left and right like dominos. Charlie knew that if they didn't escape soon, the end result would not be good. Boom! Another explosion sounded like a herd of stampede elephants. Suddenly, the cell doors containing his family and the one containing Ryan Hawking fell to the floor. Ironically, all the others remained shut. Charlie looked up and murmured a quick prayer of thanks before stuffing his slingshot back in his pocket and racing up the stairs with his family and new friend.

...

"We need to get away here!" Howled Ryan Hawking as he raced up the staircase. When they reached the top they saw Evan's troops locked in battle against American forces. Ryan realized that the Americans were here for him.

"Get to safety! Find a place to hide!" The family quickly obeyed and hid away from the ruckus. Ryan grabbed a fallen pistol and a golden sword that was on display.

Pew! Pew! He fired the pistol. He may have been locked in prison for two decades, but he hadn't lost his touch. Two soldiers locked in hand to hand combat with two Americans fell to the ground.

The soldiers looked at him in surprise. The man they were supposed to capture had just saved their lives!

"I'm on our side boys! Carl Evans is the

leader of this attack!" He explained. The two

men scoffed at him. "Yeah right. You killed

him!"

"Then why is he standing there on that balcony telling these people to kill us?" Ryan asked. The soldiers looked to the balcony and saw an older man commanding the enemy troops. Even though he was older, Ryan could tell that the soldiers knew it truly was Evans. One of them took a picture and radiod his commander, telling him the whole story and sending him the picture. The commander asked to speak to Ryan, who informed him of everything as quickly as he could. Evans. Ali. The nukes. The Boxford family. All of it.

"Well I suppose this means you're not my target. Are you ready to fight again?" Asked MaxBarley from over the radio.

"More than ready sir!" Ryan replied and kept back into the fight. Though the Americans were outnumbered three to one, it meant nothing. Evan's troops were not nearly as well trained. They put up a brave fight, but it wasn't long before the Americans began gaining ground. Ryan gunned down another soldier but suddenly the gun flew from his hands. Ali Hussein had stood behind him, holding another gold sword and a small gun.

"Mind if I cut in?" He asked.

"Certainly not!" Replied Ryan and charged towards him. *Clang!* Metal met metal time and time again. Ryan managed to smack Ali's gun away with his sword, but couldn't land a fatal blow. He parried and blocked the best he could but Ali seemed to be gaining the upper hand. Ryan was driven back into a corner and pressed up against a wall. Ali pushed his sword hard against Ryan's and Ryan found his blade inches from his neck.

"You're finished Mr. Hawking. I've looked forward to this!" He taunted.

"Well old friend, you'll have to wait longer!" Ryan scowled back and stomped on Ali's foot. The bow startled the evil man enough that Ryan managed to step out of the corner, but Ali was soon on him again. *"Zing!"* Ali managed to stab him on the left side of his stomach. Ryan screamed in agony and the sword flew from his hand and landed on the floor with a dreadful *clang!*

Ali marched towards him and raised the sword above his head. "It appears you are not the better man." He sneered. He began to bring the sword down but never finished the blow. Without warning, both of his hands flew from his body and onto the ground below. Ryan looked up to see David Boxford standing behind Ali.

"You're right. Our God, Jesus Christ is a better man." He said and jabbed the sword into Ali's chest. The evil man fell dead at his feet.

...

David sighed as he helped Ryan to his feet. He began sobbing bitterly. Not for himself, but Ali.

Ryan Hawking rubbed his shoulder. "You did what was right Mr. Boxford. And you did it well." He said empathetically.

David sighed as he wiped away his tears. "He was practically my brother."

"I know. It's extremely unfortunate. And I feel your pain Mr. Boxford. Not a day went by where I felt sad I was killing the unsaved instead of ministering to them." Ryan explained.

"But You did the right thing. We both did." Said David, his confidence and peace of mind slowly returning.

"Well is your family?" Ryan asked.
"I sent them ahead of me with the help of some troops. They're safe." David said.

"Okay good. I think we're about done here." Said Ryan.
David looked to see the Americans finish off the last of their enemies. They'd done it! They'd survived!

...

Once outside, David found Max Barkley sitting and talking with his family. He rushed forward and the family quickly embraced each other in a big group hug. It was a long time before they let each other go.

"Dad, is Mr. Hussein..." Charlie asked.

"Yes son. He is." David said somberly. His family mourned for the man who was once their friend. At least it had seemed like a real friendship. But God's ways were good and perfect and David had no doubt that God had known long before the unfortunate choices Ali Hussein had made.

Suddenly, a deep rumble sounded loudly from inside the castle. *"No, not inside the castle. In the mountain!"* David thought, suddenly alarmed. He exchanged a look with Ryan Hawking and Max Barkley.

The trio thought the same question at the same time: *"Where had Commander Evans gone?"*

17

"He was shot. Right?" Asked David, his heart now pounding like crazy.

Commander Barkley tried to radio a base in America but had no luck. "He's downed the communication system. Stay here." Commander Barkley ordered him and his family. He and his reassigning men charged back into the castle, Ryan Hawking along with them.

...

Deep within the mountain, Commander Evans had just launched the countdown for fifteen minutes to fire the nukes. So what if his troops had been defeated? His goal would still be accomplished! He could still frame the pastor for his despicable action. He could frame Max Barkley too. Nothing had changed!

...

Five minutes went by and Charlie and the rest of the Boxford family began to grow worried. The Americans should have been back by now.

David sighed and looked at his family. "Are we going to just sit here and do nothing?" The question didn't need to be answered. The Boxford family raced toward the castle.

"Some Godly family you lead! We're disobeying the orders of a military commander!" Louise joked as they rushed inside.

"God forgive us." David laughed.
The family found the troops trying to blast open a massive metallic door. But guns and even small bombs had no effect. They tried to dig under the door, but the hole wasn't big enough to house even one soldier.

"I told you and your family to stay put!" Commander Barkley hissed.

"Your country is our country sir! There must be something we can do!" His father replied.

Commander Barkley sighed and scratched his head. "I admire your patriotism sir but if you don't know how to open that door, you'll be of no help." He replied solemnly. It was then that Charlie noticed the hole. Not big enough for a soldier no, but maybe for a teenager…

"Sir! I have an idea!" He piped up. Commander Barkley eyed him suspiciously. "I can fit through that hole and reach whatever powers the nukes and destroy it!"

Commander Barkley's eyes widened in shock. "I would never allow it! You're a minor child!"

"Sir, Charlie's right!" Ceases surprised to see Marcy stand by him. "Me and him are the only one's small enough to fit through that hole!"

"But honey you and your brother may die!" Shrieked his mother.

"We just found you! We're not losing you again!" His father put in.

"Two things: One, we found you. Two, we've survived this much with God's help. He'll help us now, I know it!" Marcy explained.

Charlie's parents embraced him and his sister. "You're right. Go. But be back for supper." Their mother said.

"We will." Charlie said. *"God willing."* He added silently to himself.

Commander Barkley sighed deeply. "I'm gonna get court-martialed for this." He muttered to himself and turned to the kids. "Go. And be back quick!"

"Yes sir!" The kids said in unison and dived through the hole. It was a tight squeeze but they both made it.

Charlie turned to the door. "Push a shovel through! One of us can stay here and dig the hole big enough for you guys to fit through!" The teen didn't hear the response but a shovel was passed through to them.

He then turned to Marcy. "You have stronger arms! You stay here and dig the hole! I'll stop the nukes!"
"Evans will be there!" Marcy hissed. "What makes

you think you can stop him?!" "It's called

confidence. Have you ever heard of it?" Charlie

replied with a smile. Marcy smiled back and

grabbed the shovel. "Go on nerd. Be a hero."

"Yes ma'am!" Charlie said, an edge of sarcasm in his voice. Before Marcy could reply, he raced away.

...

Charlie wasn't that strong, but he was a great runner. He soon reached a large room filled with medieval-looking artifacts and weapons on all sides. At the front of the room was a control board. In front of it was a giant screen that read **3:00**. A second later it read:**2:59**. It was the countdown clock! Charlie didn't have much time!

Suddenly, a gust of wind out of nowhere and pushed him down on his stomach. A second later, the sound of a gunshot filled the room. Charlie raced behind the control panel for cover. He then looked up and said a quick prayer of thanks. God had rescued him again!

A strong voice echoed throughout the room: "Charlie Boxford, I would greatly appreciate it if you stepped away from the control panel." Said Chris Evans in a stern but mocking polite voice.

"Not happening!" Charlie yelled back bravely. He expected more gunshots but they didn't come. Charlie suddenly realized why. *"He can't fire at me without hitting the control panel!"*

As if the evil commander had read his thoughts, Evans growled menacingly. "Step away from the control panel boy!"

"You'll shoot me if I do!" Charlie called back.

"True, but you can't save your people by just sitting there!" Evans retorted. Charlie sighed. The evil man had a good point there. Charlie sat there panicking, trying desperately to think of a last-second plan. He came up with one idea, but it was so stupid and risky he would get himself killed in an instant. There was no way it would work. He didn't have the courage to execute it.

"It;s a shame, you know." Evans taunted him. "First your grandparents and now your country. What a sad ending for Charlie Boxford and his pathetic Christian family."

"You know about my grandparents?!" Charlie hissed in shock.

"Hussein was close with your father. He told me everything. It was your fault they died you know. I hope you know that." Evans said cruelly.
Sheer rage gave Charlie the courage he needed to put his plan into action.He made sure he was fully behind the control panel so Evans couldn't see what he was doing. He pulled the slingshot out of his pocket and placed a stone inside it. He made sure he was fully behind the control panel so Evans couldn't see what he was doing. *"God, please help me make this shot!"* He prayed, his heart, soul, and mind pounding in utter desperation.

...

Commander Evans prepared to fire his gun again from the balcony he was on but a soft *whoosh* caught him off guard. His pistol suddenly frew from his hands and onto the floor below.

...

"Yes! Thank you Lord!" Charlie screamed joyfully and grabbed a gold sword from over on the wall. He tried to lift it but it was too heavy. He heard Evans rushing down the stairs. The clock read **0:30.** He tried again. No luck. Evans ran across the room and towards the pistol. He tried again and the sword went in the air. He carried it towards the panel. One blow would destroy it. He raised it up...and dropped it. Evans grabbed the gun and pointed it at Charlie.

The man standing twenty feet away from him laughed maniacally. "It's over Charlie Boxford. Your God...is dead!" Evans screamed and pulled the trigger. But nothing happend. Evans tried again, but to no avail. Evans shook the gun in frustration and it split it two!

Charlie smiled a big smile. "God's not dead!" He snarled and raised the sword once more. And this time, the sword hovered over the control panel.

"No!" yelled Evans and raced towards him. *Whack!* Charlie brought the sword down as hard as he could. The sword remained stuck in the control panel. He had inflicted a deep blow. Evans grabbed him and threw him across the room. He then removed the sword.

Charlie looked up and saw the clock read **:05,:04,:03,:02,:01 ,:00.** Charlie's heart leapt in his throat as Evans turned to face him, an evil sneer across his face. Then to Charlie's relief, two beautiful words appeared on the screen: **LAUNCH FAILED.**

Evans marched towards him. "You thought you could stop me?" He hissed. "No boy is a match for me!"

Charlie stood to his feet, a big grin on his face. "Are you sure about that?" Charlie asked cheekily. Evans stared suspiciously at him and turned around. He whipped around to face Charlie again, bewilderment across his face.

"Wha-Wha-" He stammered.

"Boo-Yah!" Charlie shouted and dabbed in Evan's face.

"Charlie, are you serious? That is so dead!" Exclaimed a voice from behind. Charlie turned to see Marcy standing with his parents, Ryan Hawking, Max Barkley, and a bunch of US troops.

"It is not!" Charlie retorted angrily.

"Yes it-Charlie run!" Marcy screamed suddenly. Evans reached for Charlie and grabbed him.

"Stay away or the kid dies!" He growled at the rest of the heroes. Charlie kicked and squirmed feirecly. He wouldn't give up! Evans almost fell and spun around, leaving his back vulnerable. Pow! Pow! Several bullets fired by Ryan Hawking and Max Barkley laid into him and the evil man fell to the ground.

Charlie pushed the man off him and rushed toward his family who embraced him in a big group hug. The Boxford family had been through all kinds of heck, but they were alive and together again. And that was all that mattered.

18

On the plane ride back to America, the Boxford family exchanged a toast of victory with Max Barkley and Ryan Hawking.

"Cheers to a safe country!" Said Ryan.

"Cheers to a strong military!" Stated Max.

"Cheers to a family reunited!" Stated Charlie, holding his apple juice.

"And to our church, which is now safe!" Marcy added, holding her orange juice.

"And our faith which is also now safe!" Louise stated happily.

"And most of all to a God who watches over us no matter where we go!" Finished David.

After they all drank in celebration, Marcy turned to her brother. "I still don't see how anyone in their right mind could have apple juice instead of orange juice."

"Simple: It tastes better." Charlie replied.

"I say you're both wrong. Grape is the best." Said Mary's father.

"I guess I'm the only one with common sense in this family! The real champion is Mango!" Her mother put in.

"I say they're all great, but really what really hits the spot for me is some good old Apple Cider around Thanksgiving!" Ryan chimed in.

"Hey that's still Apple! I win!" Charlie shouted.

"He said apple cider Charlie. There's a difference." Marcy told him.

"It's still an apple is it not." Charlie replied cheekily.

Marcy went silent and then glared at him playfully. "Just shut up and eat your nerd juice." She stated.

"I'm not a nerd! You are!" Charlie said.

"Yeah right. You're the one who asked if we should knock on the door when we arrived at the castle." Marcy reminded him.

"And if I remember correctly, it was you who knocked, not me!" Charlie shot back.

"It was your idea!"

"And you went along with it!"

"You got me confused!"

"And now you're making excuses!"

"I am not!"

"Yes you are!"

"I am not!"

"You are too!"

"I am not!"

"You are too!"

"Enough!" Their father interrupted. "Goodness gracious, you both sound like you're five years old!" At that statement, everyone broke down laughing.

...

By the order of Max Barkley, the Boxford family and Ryan Hawking were not to mention the ordeal to anyone. Such a story could cause chaos across the United States and possibly even the world. The Christians were happy to oblige. They didn't want it to seem like they were superheroes that had fought off some great evil, when in reality, God was the one doing all the work and creating new miracles. He just did it behind the scenes.

...

The family then parted ways with Ryan Hawking, who was ready to get back to living his own life. Max Barkley had helped to clear his name. But even though Ryan lived several hours away from them, the Boxford family was already planning to spend Thanksgiving with him.

...

After church the following Sunday, Marcy and her family drove to one of their favorite places: The beach. After a fun day, the family watched the sunset as they cuddled together on one of the wooden benches on the boardwalk. There were no words needed. As she watched the beautiful and breathtaking sunset God had made, she was so glad she had accepted him as Christ and Savior. The fact that her family had survived the insane recent ordeal was truly amazing. But the fact that a God who could create such pretty and incredible things cared about her so much... Well, that was more amazing than anything!

...

Charlie was having similar thoughts. But he also remembered that his grandparents weren't there to watch the sunset with him. But instead of a deep stab of grief, Charlie felt a sense of peace. He would see them again one day. But until that day arrived, Charlie had a life to live. For Christ, that is. He found it truly remarkable that the most powerful being in the universe cared for him enough to sacrifice his only begotten son for him.

John 10:10 came to his mind: *"The thief only comes to steal, kill, and destroy. I came that they may have life, and may have it abundantly."*

Charlie was ready to live the life that God had promised to him. He knew it would be difficult at times. But he knew for a fact, especially after what he had just been through, that nothing was impossible with the help of Jesus Christ, the one true God. And that was more than enough for him.

127